CW01021653

MY TRUE COLOURS
I would love to hear your feedback.
Please review my book at Amazon.com
Simply search for books then add the
title, then press add review.
Make your comment and post.
Thank you, Hannah Francis

I really appreciate
your feedback

thanks

Hannah Francis x

My True Colours

A Mother's Strength

HANNAH FRANCIS

authorHOUSE®

AuthorHouse™ UK
1663 Liberty Drive
Bloomington, IN 47403 USA
www.authorhouse.co.uk
Phone: 0800.197.4150

© *2017 Hannah Francis. All rights reserved.*

No part of this book may be reproduced, stored in a retrieval system, or transmitted by any means without the written permission of the author.

Published by AuthorHouse 01/12/2017

ISBN: 978-1-5246-7656-8 (sc)
ISBN: 978-1-5246-7657-5 (e)

Print information available on the last page.

Any people depicted in stock imagery provided by Thinkstock are models, and such images are being used for illustrative purposes only. Certain stock imagery © Thinkstock.

This book is printed on acid-free paper.

Because of the dynamic nature of the Internet, any web addresses or links contained in this book may have changed since publication and may no longer be valid. The views expressed in this work are solely those of the author and do not necessarily reflect the views of the publisher, and the publisher hereby disclaims any responsibility for them.

Chapter 1

My mother had five children. She tragically lost her first child a daughter at eighteen months of age. The child was born with spina bifida, and she contracted meningitis at ten days old, leaving her blind. She had meningitis again at eighteen months, which ended her short life.

My parents went on to have four healthy children. My sister Sophie was followed by my brother, Andrew. Then she went in to have her fourth child, and she came out of hospital with two. That was lucky for me because I was the second twin to enter the world. They were thrilled. Mam always told me that God gave her one back. Dad was relieved because this stopped her craving for more children. She named us Lauren and Lorna.

My father always said that if his dad had lived long enough to see us, then we would have been ruined. Sophie was the apple of his eye, and losing his first granddaughter had broken his heart. Dad was extremely proud of producing twins and often felt the need to tell us that when we were conceived, they did it in the night and in the morning! Who wants to hear about your conception when you're five?

Lorna and I were very close growing up. Dad always remarked that he could put money on me entering the room first, and Lorna would soon follow in my footsteps. I was the strong-willed twin and grew up to be overbearingly protective of Lorna. This used to annoy her. I was always the one who wanted to go on an adventure, whereas Lorna was afraid to try anything new. This meant I was the one who always got into trouble. One day a few of us were playing on one of our friends' dad's work lorries. He came out to shout at us to get down, everyone else jumped off before me. When I jumped off, I got my knickers hooked on the lorry, leaving me hanging there. Eventually after much wriggling, they tore into shreds, leaving me lying on the ground with scratched knees and a bare bum. Worse still, Mam had insisted on us wearing her favourite outfit, a polo neck jumper. We had several shades with the petticoat pleated skirts. They were short as hell, and this resulted in me having to walk home with my bare bum showing. Lorna had stayed on the bank, watching us, because she was too scared to get onto the lorry.

That was the beginning of how life went for us. Lorna played it safe and got away with everything. She was never bullied. On the other hand, I was too busy fighting both our battles, keeping us safe, and having fun. It was safe to say Lorna became the popular twin. She was also judged the pretty twin by all, with exception to my grandfather and my dad, who always argued that I would blossom later on in life. I was the ugly duckling!

The one thing that was positive about Lorna's laid-back approach to life was that it meant that I got away with most things; she always gave into my demands, which was great.

When we were young, our parents bought a shop and transformed it into a chip shop. However, because of the potato crisis, apparently we had such bad weather that the price of potatoes went up to seven pounds a sack! Back then, that was a lot of money, which meant that they had to close the shop and rent it out to a Chinese family. The village had a new Chinese takeaway.

Mam said she was pleased; she hated the bloody place. It must have been bad because she never swore. She said that she was bringing up us four, running a chip shop in the evenings, and coping with a mother-in-law with depression. I knew then that she must be a saint.

After the chippy closed, we all went to live with our nan – yes, the one with depression. She hated me, and I didn't like her much either. Granddad had passed away a few years earlier, before Andrew, Lorna, and I were born. Sophie had been the apple of his eye and therefore was also hers. This gave her automatic rights to any decent jewellery and pocket money. Andy and Lorna were also given pocket money, and Nan would hand out ten pence to them and they'd run to the shop. I'd always be left behind with my hand out, waiting for her to unburden her bulging purse with my ten pence. She'd rummage around, pull out two pence, and begrudgingly put it in my hand. Every time it was two bloody pence.

Good old Mam would hunt around the cushions of the settee and get it up to ten pence for me, always reminding me that she was giving me her last. I knew she was, but when you're a kid, you don't care about that. Anyway, my logic was that she should shout at Nan for being so mean. Mam never would; she was far too polite and would never cheek her elders. My mother was brought up properly and used to tell me she was taught to have good manners and respect elders.

Chapter 2

My mother's parents were old when they started a family. Mam was born when Nan was forty, and her brother came along four years later. I think she thought she was on the menopause, but my uncle arrived. I always thought that was a pity, really. I didn't like him and used to wish the menopause had arrived instead. Nan and Granddad were really old when we were kids, and they both died before Lorna and I reached the age of ten. I can remember their house. It was old-fashioned but clean and tidy. It had a musky smell, and Nan always wore a crossover pinny. They had honeysuckle bushes growing in the front garden and gooseberry bushes in the long back garden. As I approached the house, which was on the top of a steep hill, I could smell the honeysuckle. Mam always made us smell it because she loved the scent.

Nan was an excellent cook. There were always fruit tarts and cakes on the table. I can remember sitting on her lap and touching her cheek; it was like a peach, and I used to ask her how her skin was so soft. She told me that she always washed her face in cold water. I have copied her ever since. We were six years old then. I liked my mother's mam and she liked me.

Mam said that Granddad must have had a soft spot for me and Lorna because he kept a photo of us in his wallet. We were the only twins in the family. Mam was never his favourite; he doted on her elder sister. He always told Mam that when she was a child, they'd leave her in the garden to scare away the crows, whereas he always had to be careful with her sister because she was so pretty someone may try to steal her. This understandably left Mam with little confidence. I don't think he ever knew how much that hurt her as a child. She never got over it, and it affected her for her whole life.

My mother was a kind, loving person. She doted on us and Dad. She enjoyed the household chores as much as anyone could, and although she didn't have new furniture, it was of good quality and our home was spotless. Her children, her husband, and her home were her main priorities, and in that order – and Dad knew it. They never argued as such, but they bickered constantly, usually about silly things. We always had food on the table, a warm bed, and a great Christmas.

Dad used to say that if Mam ran out of potatoes and eggs, and if the tin opener broke, we would starve to death. Occasionally the posh relations from Dad's side would surprise us with a visit, giving my mother a day's notice of arrival. Dad would tell them that was the only time she spring cleaned. Mam would be fuming! It was funny, though: he was a joker and everyone knew it. Everyone dreaded the constant onslaught of jokes, and if anyone in the room laughed, we were done for because he'd reel them off all night.

During the holidays, Lorna and I had great fun. I was starting to get her to be a little more adventurous, and we were climbing trees and going on adventures, exploring the fields and the park behind our house. It was a recreational grounds, and there were tennis courts and a bowling alley there for the older people. We had great fun on our bikes and played tennis on warm, sunny days. We started making friends and would be out all day. Mam didn't mind; she was glad to get us from under her feet.

We became friends with a girl called Lucy. Lucy lived with her brothers and her dad; her mam had left them all for another man. I could understand why because her dad was weird and had a funny accent. Lucy said he was brought up in Kent.

We didn't like her dad and could tell the feeling was mutual. We would meet Lucy at the tennis courts, and because there were three of us, we had to take turns playing. One would be ball girl and wait on the sidelines, like in Wimbledon. One day a man approached us, and he said he was the park keeper. At first we thought we had done something wrong, but he said that he had been watching us for a while and wondered if we would like to go see his collection of birds; he had an aviary on the grounds, and he told us all the local children were allowed to visit. We thanked him, and he walked away then turned around and waved at us. He seemed like a friendly man. When we told Mam about it the next day, she didn't seem happy about it but wouldn't say why. We started to visit the birds and reassured Mam that it was OK, because the man had a son, a girlfriend, and a baby granddaughter living there as well. They were really nice, and the baby was lovely; we used to play with her.

The park keeper's name was Vic. Going to see the birds became a daily event, and it meant that even on rainy days, we could go out. Mam didn't like Vic or the fact that we were always up there, and she wondered why he didn't mind. He made an effort to befriend my parents by planting spare flowers in the garden for them, but she wasn't convinced. I overheard her talking to Dad one evening. "I don't know about that guy. Why does he want young girls up his house all the time? It isn't right." Dad told her to stop worrying because Vic seemed OK. We agreed with Dad. What was she concerned about?

About six months later, Vic went away on holiday to Belgium with his friend. When he came back, he gave us some chocolates, and we shared them out between the three of us. I thought they were OK, but personally I preferred Cadburys.

Vic started to get more birds. He bought lovebirds, and they were pretty. He explained that they couldn't live on their own because they had to have a mate. He also bought a chinchilla; it was so soft and cute, and all three of us would race up to see it every day after school. It was only a baby, and we loved him and called him Harry. It was like having our own pet shop. Mam was scared of birds and rodents of any kind, so we knew we wouldn't be allowed any of these pets in the house. We had a dog, but she was old and boring in comparison. The aviary was an old greenhouse at the back of Vic's house and doubled as a den. We loved going there because we could do anything. He used to give Lorna and Lucy fags, but I didn't like smoking. He let us try alcohol as well, but I didn't like it; it was lager and tasted disgusting.

When it was raining, in order to kill the boredom, Vic started suggested we play games like I spy or hide and seek. This started to become a routine. Sometimes he would find us straight away, and other times he'd take ages.
When he found us, he thought it was funny to tickle us. If I was hiding in an awkward place, he would help me down, sometimes touching me in my private place. Sometimes he'd slap me on the bum as a joke. I didn't think anything of it. It was Vic, and he was only messing about. Life went on as normal, and we were eleven years old.

Lorna and I were preparing to start comprehensive school. We had our new uniform and were telling Vic all about the visits to our new school. He started to complain that we would forget about him and get boyfriends. I thought, *Well, yeah. What's the big deal?* I thought it was an odd comment. The next day, I went up to feed the birds before Lorna; she didn't feel well but said she might come up later. I was there for about an hour when Vic arrived. I was telling him that I'd fed the chinchilla. I was looking at the lovebirds, checking whether they needed water. Vic started to tickle me. I tried to pull away but was laughing at the same time. He then tried to pull up my skirt and grab at my groin. He held me tight, put his mouth to my ear, and said, "I can't wait to fuck you."

I could feel the bile rising in my throat, and I somehow managed to scrabble free and run home, terrified. I ran upstairs, sat on the bed, and felt numb. Suddenly everything was sinking in. The tickling games were rude, naughty, and disgusting, but I hadn't understood. Still, I knew what those words meant. I felt sick to the pit of my stomach, and most of all I felt dirty.

Mam entered the bedroom and asked if I was OK. I told her Lorna and I had argued. This was my secret – I couldn't tell her or anyone because I felt so ashamed. Lorna and Lucy came to look for me, and I told them what had happened. Lucy said he had touched her as well when we were playing hide and seek. She said we should tell someone. I replied, "No way!" The thought of anyone else knowing was too much. I swore them both to secrecy that day, telling them that if they told anyone, I would kill myself. I meant it, and they both knew it. This changed me forever.

Chapter 3

Lorna and Lucy continued to visit the birds. I begged them not to go, but Lucy didn't care; I think she liked the attention. Her father never bothered with her at home, and her brothers were older than her and busy with school and girlfriends. Lorna told me he never touched her, and I believed her. Nothing ever happened to her – it was always me. I wondered, *Why me? What is wrong with me?* Lorna didn't understand what I was going through. She used to ask me to go back up there with them, and I'd tell her, "No fucking way!"

The thought of it used to make me feel sick, but I also worried that I couldn't protect Lorna. She didn't care about me or what I was feeling. She said he was asking about me all the time. I would tell her to shut up because I didn't care, and I wished he'd drop dead. Lorna still didn't get it. I'd beg her and Lucy to stay away from there, but they wouldn't listen; the free fags were too much temptation. This meant that I spent most of my evenings and weekends alone. I decided that I didn't want any new friends anyway.

I felt like a freak and was afraid that they might sense that I was weird and so scared that everyone could tell what had happened to me.

My parents concluded that I had hit the stroppy teenager age early, and this was their explanation for my odd behaviour. My dad used to work weekends on a market stall, selling curtains and cushions, and we had to help out. This was the only time I left the house apart from going to school. The stallholders were friendly enough and gave each other discounts on goods.

The long summer days on the market were busy, and I used to observe people and wonder how girls could have boyfriends. Surely they didn't want boys to touch them. I concluded that my mother must have wanted children really badly to do that! How she managed it four times with my dad amazed me. I'd watch the young girls going into the backs of vans with the market stallholders and having love bites all over their necks. They were disgusting, just sluts. I warned my dad if I ever saw him talking to those girls, I'd tell Mam.

Dad always said there was no harm in looking so long as he didn't touch; that was his humour, but I'd call him a pervert. I didn't mind Dad, and he was quite funny – so long as he didn't touch me at all. I was fourteen years old.

School was a chore. Lorna mixed in well with her classmates. We were separated as soon as we started the comprehensive; the teachers thought it would help us to grow as individuals. Lorna had loads of friends. I found it hard and preferred spending time alone; it gave me time to think about things. Lorna would always look for me at lunchtime, and her friends were nice enough, but I was in a higher set and was alone during class time. I quickly learned to stop fighting in the comp because my arch-enemy from junior school had three older sisters who attended the same school, and she was chomping at the bit to fight me, knowing they would by waiting on the sidelines to join in. My excuse was that she should grow because up fighting was for kids, and I was past all that now. They were the school bullies, and everyone hated them but was too afraid to admit it.

I hated my classmates because they were snobs. The girls from my junior school often commented that I was like a lost sheep without Lorna by my side. They were right: she was my safety blanket. When she was there, I didn't need friends and only needed her. However, Lorna didn't need me and flourished on her own. She was nice and always was the popular twin. I was the freak. I styled my hair so it was spiky and wore make-up to school. I had my own style, and I loved it. My weekly pay from the markets went towards a good haircut and clothes. I saved for everything, whereas Lorna spent her pay on fags and the fruit machines. My hair was my crowning glory. I could do anything with it, and it was nearly black and shone. I'd sit in the bedroom, blow-dry my hair, and practice putting on make-up to perfection. I started to enjoy my job at the market because it got me out of the house on the weekends. Due to Lorna's nagging, I had started bothering with Lucy and her stepsister Jenny; we used to hang around with a mixed crowd of different aged kids every evening.

Dad had the opportunity to work for three days in Camarthan. Andy and I had to go, and it would mean sleeping in the van. Dad said he needed the help and would pay us extra if we went. He explained that it was an opportunity to make good money because it was a big event and would attract a lot of potential customers. We arrived on the Friday and set up the stall. I had a look around: it was just a huge field. After breakfast, I went on the hunt for the ladies. Eventually, I found a hut with a woman on the door. As I pushed the door open, I could see cobwebs everywhere and fat black spiders on the ceiling and walls. No fucking way was I going in there.

When I got back to the stall, I was now desperate for the loo and explained the situation to Dad. He told me not to worry because he would set up a curtain. I could go behind the stall, and no one would see me. Ten minutes later, the job was done, and I was so relieved! After sorting myself out, I got back out to the stall. The next thing I heard was my dad shouting, "What the fuck is that smell?" He then realised that it was behind the curtain. He shouted, "I didn't think you needed a shit! That's going to stink all fucking day!" If I could have made a wish that day, it would have been for the ground to open up and swallow me. Andy thought it was funny – until he was told to throw a box over it. I turned on my heels and walked away. I had never been shamed so badly. I hated my dad for shouting, Andy for laughing, and everyone in the whole world that day.

After returning several hours later and sending them both to Coventry, I stayed in the van. I was not serving customers or facing anyone after that. How the fuck was I to know he thought I wanted a pee? I didn't want food or drink, or to see anyone. Dad came around and thought it was hilarious. He tried to bribe me out of the van with food and drink, but I politely told him to piss off because I was never speaking to him again! One thing Mam had over him: she didn't scrape arse. If you refused to eat your food, she left you to sulk until you came around.

Another embarrassing moment from my market days happened when I used to work on Sundays. The summers were always hot and humid, so I used to take a change of clothes. My mother had been brought up by old parents and so would not let us shave our legs. I was around the age of fifteen. We could use Immac, but this stank and was messy to apply. Besides, I had ran out of it several weeks ago. I was not expecting such a hot weekend. I arrived at the market with jeans on, and as the morning wore on, the temperature soared to sweltering. I decided to change into my shorts, which were in the van. Although this was a good idea, I hadn't shaved my legs. I thought, *OK, I will go to the local chemist, buy a razor and shaving cream, and shave them in the toilets.* Looking back, I should have changed back into my jeans first. After several comments of "Is your dad a mammoth?" and "All right, furry?" while en route to the chemist, I got to the toilets to shave my legs. I walked back to the stall with cleanly shaven, razor-cut, white legs. With an "I don't give a fuck what you think" attitude, I strutted back to the stall with as much confidence as I could muster. The joys of being a teenager!

I hated school and was bullied and called names daily by most of the class. I didn't care because I hated them all. I had been wearing a brace for eighteen months, I have sucked my thumb when I sleep since I was little and this had pushed my teeth forward. I asked the dentist for the brace as I was very concious of my teeth looking crooked. This gave them ammunition. I got called ugly, jaws, and spastic. They were so fucking childish. One day as I entered my chemistry lesson and took my usual seat. The ringleader, a nasty bitch called Sarah, told me to move. I replied, "Fuck off!" The teacher still hadn't arrived, so she had time to continue with the usual onslaught of names. I snapped that day, grabbing her by the hair and swinging her around. I was just about to knee her in the face when the teacher arrived and screamed at me to put her down. I was told to go to my head of year.

When he called me into his office, I broke down crying and told him everything about the bullying and name calling. I begged him to move me to the same class as my sister, saying that I hated all my classmates. He told me to go back to class and assured me he was going to look into it.

My chemistry teacher and head of year had a chat at the end of the lesson outside the door. They asked me to stay behind so that she could have a word with me. I was dreading it because she was one of the strictest teachers in the school. When she came into the classroom, she asked me, "How long has this been going on?" I told her, and she said, "Why didn't you say something?" I told her I just had and started to cry. She told me to stop crying, don't let them beat me, and stay strong. I learned a valuable lesson that day.

The next day I moved to Lorna's class. School began to improve. I was in the lower set, but I didn't care – I fit in. Lorna and I chose different options and therefore were only in a few lessons together, but I had a few friends now, and my confidence grew. I didn't know what pop groups I liked except for Wham, so I copied the names from a few of the other girls' books so that mine looked the same. I was good at English, typing, and cookery, but I hated maths and was rubbish at it. I had to do RE because it was a Catholic school. I didn't mind it, though; I believed there was a God and went to church every Sunday. Lorna didn't go to church or communion, and she didn't believe in God. I didn't understand her; people needed to believe in something, didn't they?

Chapter 4

We went out after school most evenings but had to be in at 9:30, or else our parents would come looking for us. This was embarrassing because most of the group were allowed out much later. Mam was strict, which was annoying. There was a mixed crowd of friends, and some of the girls were pairing off with the nicer-looking boys. The boys seemed to change girlfriends all the time. I didn't know who was with who half of the time. Some of the girls were constantly covered in love bites, and it was disgusting. We saved our money for the weekends. One of the boys' parents went out on Fridays, so we went to his house. We clubbed our money together, and the eldest of the group, who was nearly eighteen and shaving, could get served in the local shop. We put in our orders; it was either sherry or Strongbow.

I usually had some sherry because I didn't mind the taste of it, and it didn't smell as bad as Strongbow. Lorna and I had chewing gum to hide the scent of drink and her fags for when we got home. (Yes, 9.30 on the weekends as well – we were sixteen)! Some of the girls slept around with the older boys, wore miniskirts, and flirted with anything in trousers. Lorna was yet again more popular than me with everyone because she smoked and was funny.

Lorna likes one of the lads, Carl. She has arranged to see him the next weekend. She is trying to get me to have a date with his friend. Lorna says he's a good laugh, and I shouldn't be tight, but I don't want to. He constantly takes the piss out of everything I say, and he's covered in zits. I don't like him, but they are friends. Sometimes I think that she cares more about pleasing her friends than me.

I decide to stay in for a few weeks. I have GCSE coursework in English to do, and it's my favourite subject. We are the first year to do a GCSE exam. I find it easier doing coursework; it is going towards my final exam, and I want to pass it. Lorna goes out every night as usual and can't be bothered to revise or do her homework. She starts asking our parents if our friends can come to the house some evenings, because it's winter and too cold to hang around outside. We have a large back kitchen dinner, and Mam says that they can go in there as long as they are quiet. It's a bit awkward, because I live there but do not go downstairs and say hello. Carl's friend Zitty is there, and he is being nice to me for a change. He asks me why I haven't been going out lately. I reply that I am doing homework for my exams.

When the weather breaks, I start to go out with Lorna again. It's boring, but there's nothing else to do. Zitty talks to me quite often now, and I suppose he's OK; maybe he's growing up a bit. Lorna's boyfriend Carl asks if Zitty can walk me down the hill on the way home, I cringe and say no, Lorna tells me not to be tight because Carl is walking down with her, and they are going the same way anyway. I think, *Fucking great. Thanks, Lorna.* Realising I don't really have a choice, I agree. We talk a little bit on the way home, and he's OK as boys go. When we get to the bus stop near the house, Lorna is French kissing Carl. Gross! Zitty asks if he can walk me down tomorrow, and for some stupid reason, I feel sorry for him and so agree.

Chapter 5

Three months later, Lorna is still with Carl, and I'm still seeing Zitty. We are going to a friend's house whose parents are away for the weekend. She's a right slapper, but her sister is hard as nails, a slapper as well and three years older than us, so we say nothing. A free house is a free house, so who are we to complain? Besides, it's raining out, and it beats the bus stop (my and Zitty's dating zone). I have my bottle of QC sherry for tonight; Lorna is on the Strongbow. We get to the house, and everyone is there. Lisa, whose house it is, is strutting around and looking for her next victim. Lorna is with Carl and is on her second can already. I'm drinking my QC.

As the night wears on, I notice Lisa and Zitty flirting. I think, *The cheeky bitch,* but I say nothing. I notice Lorna and Carl have gone upstairs. In order to piss off Lisa, I tell Zitty we should do the same. I've had a few drinks, and the Dutch courage has kicked in. I don't think this through. We head upstairs, and the room is a bit messy. I lie on the bed, and Zitty undresses us both. I am nervous, and he's clumsy;

whatever he's trying to do hurts like hell. Both Lorna and I lose our virginity that night. On the way home, Lorna says she doesn't care and is relieved she's done it and isn't a virgin anymore. I'm upset and don't even know why I did it; I didn't like it and won't be doing it again.

Several weeks later Lorna and Carl split up. Neither of them are that bothered. Carl takes magic mushrooms all the time and is more interested in doing that than seeing her. I'm still with Zitty, and we get on OK and meet most nights. We have sex occasionally if we have somewhere to go. I feel that because I lost my virginity to him, I have to stay with him. I can't stand the thought of being branded a slag, like some of the girls.

School is finished, and I have decided to go to college to complete a secretarial B.Tech degree. It is for a year, and I am going to look for office work after that. Zitty is working in a factory, and his wages are crap. Lorna has also started in a factory; she makes underwear and has made loads of new friends. She's dating a new fella named John, and he's into his heavy metal bands. Lorna suddenly loves all heavy metal bands, and she is going to a Donnington Festival and booking tickets for John's favourite groups.

I am seventeen years old and have been dating Zitty for a year. We get engaged (his idea). I am about to finish college, have nearly completed my course, and manage to make a few of my own friends. Beth comes into college the following week and announces that she is pregnant and engaged. We ask if she's OK and how her parents were about it. She tells us the engagement was rushed due to the pregnancy, but she will get married after she has had the baby. She's happy, so we congratulate her. Three days later, I discover I am also pregnant by Zitty. Shit! Later that night, I tell him. He is OK about it. He tells me he hates living at home, and this will be a good excuse to move out. He hates his stepdad. I decide I have to tell Mam first; she loves kids and will take it better than Dad. Looking on the positive side, at least I have completed my college course.

A few days later, I think, *Here goes. Mam's on her own.* I start by saying, "Um, Mam?"

She replies, "Yes?"

I then say, "Oh, nothing."

After the same conversation five times, she says, "Lauren, you're pregnant, aren't you?"

My lip quivers, and I reply yes and start to cry. Mam is my rock. She tells me it will be OK and that she will tell Dad. I'm so relieved. I go out and come back home several hours later.

As I walk into the kitchen, I see my father at the table. I ask if he's OK. He shouts, "No, I'm fucking not OK!" I start to cry. Dad asks me what my plans are and says I can get rid of it, if it's not too late. I tell him I'm Catholic and can't kill it. He shouts at me to get to bed. I run up the stairs and cry myself to sleep.

The next day, Dad has come around a little; I think Mam gave him a row. He's not happy, but he's not angry anymore. He tells me that I will have to live at home with the baby if I'm going to have it. I've brought enough shame on the family, and there is no way I'm moving out unless I have a ring on my finger. I tell Zitty what has been said. He comes to the house and tells Dad that we should get married. The wedding is arranged to happen after the birth of the baby.

Throughout the pregnancy, Zitty becomes more and more moody. I am terrified of being left as a single mother. I can't bear the thought of people thinking I'm a slag. Zitty starts arguments all the time, and he gets nasty and jealous of any other man talking to me. I put up with the jealously and comments about being fat. He only says nasty things when we are alone. He acts as nice as pie in front of my family. Sophie picks up on his behaviour and watches his jealous mood swings; they quickly fall out, and he hates her. I'm in the middle of the arguments. He has power, and he knows it.

Chapter 6

The months roll by, and I get fatter as my pregnancy progresses. Lorna is having the time of her life; she and John have split up, and she is going on holidays with the girls from work. She has booked Magalof. Lorna and Zitty get on well, and he goes out sometimes and sees her in the same pubs. They both smoke and go out for a fag together. Zitty won't let anyone smoke in front of me and is protective of my pregnancy. He uses it as an excuse to stop me going out or seeing friends, making me feel guilty if I want to go anywhere. He's living his life, and I have become a hermit!

Lorna comes in from work and tells me that the girls in the factory said to tell me that labour is like trying to shit a melon. I shout to Mam and ask her if it's true. Mam gives Lorna a row and tells me I can expect some twinge pains, but that's all. I'm terrified!

A month later, the baby is on its way. We head to the local hospital. The doctor informed me a few months ago that the baby was in a back-to-back position. Mam and I don't know what that means. The pains are getting worse. I'm so scared and terrified of soiling myself because I know Zitty will tell everyone. Luckily, they give me an enema, which clears my bowels like an explosion! Thirty-six hours later, after pain that could kill a horse (I thought I was going to die), Jonah has arrived. He's a healthy, seven-pound boy.

Three days later, it is my and Lorna's eighteenth birthday. Zitty visits me in hospital, and every time he looks at the baby, he comments how much he looks like him. Jonah does a little, but a handsome version. I am grateful that he doesn't have Zitty's nose. My parents arrive to view the new arrival; he is the first grandchild on both sides. Mam is instantly smitten, as am I. Dad takes a peek and smiles, commenting, "Yep, ten fingers and toes. You did OK."

My parents go for a coffee, leaving me and Zitty alone with our son. I sense a change of mood in Zitty. He comments that my mam should ask before picking up Jonah, and that it's his child. I tell him he's being silly, and he should be grateful – we'd have nothing if it wasn't for them. He looks down at Jonah but doesn't pick him up, and I can tell he's angry. I ask him what's wrong. He tells me that I am a fucking slut and asks why I allowed a male student to observe the birth and stitch me up. I'm shocked and stare at him. Eventually I ask him, "What is the problem? They are doctors." he pinches my arm hard, and I start to cry and can't stop. He's telling me to shut up because someone might hear me.

A nurse approaches and asks if I'm OK. he panics and tries to offer an explanation. The nurse says, "It's nothing to worry about – just the baby blues. Every mother gets them." As she walks away, I look up and see the relief on his face. My parents come back from the canteen, and Zitty comments about the baby blues. Mam comforts me.

Eventually visiting time is over, and they leave. I look at Jonah and decide I don't care anymore. Lorna hasn't come to visit us; Mam said she would come around, and she thinks that she's jealous of the attention I am getting. I was in hospital on our birthday, and no one had any cash left to celebrate it with her. My parents assumed she would be going out with her friends. (I don't think she ever forgave me.)

Five days after giving birth, I leave hospital and go home to live at my parents' house. Zitty visits daily, using Jonah as an emotional weapon against anyone who crosses him, usually Sophie. They hate each other, but Sophie adores her nephew. She is extremely broody and smothers him with affection. I don't condone Zitty's behaviour, but occasionally it gives me some breathing space.

I decided to breastfeed, because this is the only thing that no one can do for me. Jonah is the only grandchild on both sides, and everyone wants to spoil him. He is picked up constantly, which is annoying. Mam coos over him, saying, "Come to Mam." I have to correct her that she is Nan. Dad reminds me that I cannot move out unless I am married. I think, *Zitty only wants to marry me to piss off everyone.* I only want to marry him so that I can have my own space and be a real mother to Jonah. The house is too small, and I feel suffocated. Mam is brilliant and means well, but the constant comments of "I'd bring him up for you" from both grandmothers is getting me down. No one is taking him away from me – he is my son. Getting married to Zitty is my only option.

Chapter 7

The wedding is booked for three months after Jonah's birth. My baby weight is coming off quickly due to the breastfeeding. Mam had been saving for new wardrobes, but the wedding had to take priority, so her savings go towards having a dress made for me. Sophie told me she is being a bridesmaid and quickly takes over all the wedding plans. I don't care, really. I turn up for my dress fittings when asked. I have no interest in the wedding at all; Jonah is my priority. We were offered a council house about two miles away from home and are due to pick up the keys in a few days.

Mam offers to babysit whenever I need her to, because I have to go decorate the house. We are given a grant for paint so we can freshen the place up. We have no furniture except for a settee, a table, and some rickety chairs, which are given to us. Zitty helps with the decorating, but he is a liability and usually makes a mess. I arrive at the house one day, hoping he has finished painting the living room. As I open the front door, he proudly shows me the windowsill he had stripped of paint, gouged grooves in, and stained. I think, *Fucking hell, what a twat.* We now have one odd windowsill. He proudly tells me that it has taken him all day to do it. I reply, "Oh, well done. It looks great." I am pissed off but want to keep the peace. He comments that he was good at carpentry in school. Whoopee, a stained windowsill!

The wedding is a week away. I tell my parents that I will visit every day. Mam is upset that we are moving out, and she keeps telling me that I can pull out if I decide it is not what I want. Sophie always adds her comment to the conversation. Lorna is not bothered, but she has grown fond of Jonah.

The wedding day comes and goes. The day after, I arrive at my parents' for Sunday lunch, leaving Zitty in bed with a hangover. I insist on having Jonah on my wedding night. He is my son – and the best excuse I had for not having to have sex with Zitty. We acquire a bed on the wedding day, but it has no legs on it; one of the guests offered it to us because he was throwing it away. Zitty and his friends go get it after the food and speeches, and they set it up before we get home. Mam asks where my husband is, and I tell her he is in bed. She asks if I am going to cook him Sunday dinner. I reply no; there is no food in the house, anyway. He goes down to his mam's because he is an only child and is spoilt rotten, which suits me.

I soon discover my husband has no intention of working, unless it is on the fiddle. He complains that it isn't worth him working. He gets to know a few local builders from the pub, and he labours for them. He tells me he is getting around twenty quid a day. Any money he earns, he keeps for himself. He is out of my way, so I don't care. He goes to the pub every night and comes in at all hours.

Although I do not like living with my new husband, I love the independence of moving out of my parents' home. Finally I can be a proper mother to Jonah.

I promise to visit my parents every day and fit in a few visits a week to my in-laws.

The evenings are my time with Jonah. My daily routine consists of cleaning the house in the morning and visiting my parents or my mother-in-law in the day. Then I head home around five to cook tea and bathe the baby. My favourite night is Saturday. My favourite series, *Pride and Prejudice,* is on, and I love period dramas. This is just television, though, and I know there is no Mr Darcy for me. He doesn't exist in the real world.

Although Jonah is a pleasant child, he doesn't sleep. At fourteen months of age, he still has me up throughout the night. I am exhausted. Zitty never gets up with him; he is always hung-over and sleeps in on the weekends until midday. Jonah has a favourite toy, a stacking pole with colourful rings that have to be stacked onto the pole in the right order. One morning I carry Jonah into the bedroom with the toy and leave him playing on the floor while I sort the ironing. Zitty is still sleeping off his hang-over. As I turn around, I see Jonah swinging the pole part of the toy in his hand, and he smashes it down into his dad's nose. Zitty starts to groan in pain. Before he can get up, I grab Jonah and run down the stairs. Zitty is right behind me. I jump onto the settee and hold Jonah underneath me. Zitty punches my back and arms, trying to hit the baby. I scream at him to stop it, telling him it was an accident and Jonah's only a baby. He is furious that his nose is bleeding. He goes to the bathroom to get some tissue, and as he leaves the room, I grab Jonah and run out of the door. Jonah is crying and terrified. I haven't had time to get his coat on, and it's freezing out. I cuddle him to me and run to my parents' house. As I enter, they look puzzled. Jonah has calmed down now. I ask, "Can I come home?"

I have been at my parents for about a week. The news from my mother-in-law is that Zitty is devastated. She tells me he can't eat or sleep. I don't give a shit, to be honest. After a week of living at my parents' I feel like the house is closing in on me. Sophie doesn't leave Jonah alone, and we have to share a double bed with Lorna. Mam means well but is taking over again. Dad says that I can't go back and live on my own. They don't know the whole story; I told them that we had an argument. Lorna and Andy are the only ones who give me space. Andy stays at his girlfriend's house most nights. Lorna has grown to love Jonah, but only as long as he doesn't mess up her stuff or interfere with her busy social life; she's out most nights with the girls and is having a great time.

Sophie comes in one night and is drunk. She decides to put Jonah into her bed, and he starts crying. I wake up and am furious. This has made my mind up. I want to give Jonah some routine, and I feel suffocated again. I can't do this at my parents' house, and I am going back to the house. Zitty is always out, anyway. I need my own place.

The next day I go back to the house, and there are dishes everywhere. So much for the not eating. Zitty comes downstairs and is surprised to see me. I tell him I'll come back, but if he touches Jonah, I'm off – and this time I will tell my dad what really happened. Zitty's afraid of him, and this makes him agree. My parents are upset and worried about me going back to Zitty. I reassure them that I'm all right.

There is no food left at the house, so I give Zitty a tenner and tell him to go to the shop for some food. He comes back with bread, milk, eggs, and potatoes. He keeps the change, but I didn't expect any because this is routine. Any money he can get his hands on is spent in the pub. I don't care; I simply want him out of the house. An hour later, I am alone watching television, and the baby is in bed. We have our house back; it's just me and Jonah again. I realise I have to tolerate Zitty because my parents will not let me live on my own. I desire this most of all, my independence. I am nearly twenty years of age!

Chapter 8

Zitty works most days now. This is good because I don't see him. I have to claim income support because he will not get a proper job or provide for us. He has started to get into fights at the pub and has some fines. He hides letters behind the washing machine, thinking I won't see them. I read them and discover he has to go to court. His mother is ashamed, and his stepdad has the cheek to say that he was never in trouble until he got married.

Jonah is two years old, but Zitty doesn't bother with him. My mother notices and comments on it all the time. Mam says she could cry for the baby when Jonah walks up and talks to him, and Zitty simply gets up and walks away. Everyone else spoils Jonah, and I worry that he will end up like his dad if he is an only child. I cannot bear the thought of having children by different dads, so I decide I will have one more child with Zitty, and then I'm off.

It takes about six months for me to get pregnant. Zitty can't believe his luck because sex is pretty much on tap at the moment. Well, he'd better not get used to that! I usually face the wall because I don't really want to be that close to his face.

I am getting really worried that I may not be able to have any more children. I had pelvic inflammatory disease after having Jonah, and the doctor asked me about my sex life. I explained that I have only ever had one partner, and I'm married. He couldn't understand how I had contracted the disease, I explained that I had the coil fitted after having Jonah, and I think that was the cause. A month later, I discover I am pregnant. It surprises me that Zitty is pleased.

Six months into the pregnancy, I am absolutely huge, Zitty keeps commenting on how fat I am, but I don't answer back. I know he is looking for an excuse to start an argument, and I won't give him one. I make sure Zitty never has Jonah on his own; he has become ill-tempered and has no patience with him. Another court date has been set for Zitty. Now he regularly gets into fights when he's out drinking. A month later, his mother is ashamed because he is sentenced to six weeks in prison. She knows it will be in the local paper, and everyone will know; she reads the paper regularly for gossip about everyone else.

Zitty has been told that he will only do three weeks of his sentence if he behaves. I think that is wrong – six weeks should be six weeks! He makes sure that we have a phone line fitted in the house. I am nearly eight months pregnant, he tells me he will ring me every night. I know this is to make sure I don't go anywhere, and he can check that I'm home. Everyone else thinks he's worried about me. I don't know what he thinks I am going to do in my condition!

Three weeks later, Zitty is home, and I am in labour. The midwife has commented that it must be a boy because they are lazy. Zitty has refused to come in with me; his excuse is he has to work! He works (still on the fiddle) for his uncle, who would give him time off to see his child being born, but Zitty has said that he can't go through that again. Fourteen hours later, I have a second son and call him Eligh. We had an agreement that I would name the baby if it was a boy, and he would name it Polly if it was a girl. I get my way. Eligh is a healthy eight pounds, nine ounces and has black hair.

Everyone comments on what a beautiful baby Eligh is, and I have to agree. Even Zitty is smitten. I only breastfeed him for a week because he has extremely hard gums, and my nipples are cracked and really sore. I lose the baby weight quickly and am back in my size ten jeans within two weeks. It takes time to get into a routine with two children. Jonah loves his baby brother; he is nearly three and will be starting nursery school soon.

A few months later, we are lucky enough to be offered a three-bedroom house nearer to both our parents' homes. We move with the help of my family. The only problem is that the house is about five doors away from my nosey in-laws; even Zitty isn't happy about it. He and his mother share the same volatile personality and argue a lot. His stepdad spends his time spying with his binoculars on the neighbours – which will now include us! Another favourite hobby of theirs is listening in to the police radio station.

Our new home is near the nursery which Jonah is about to attend. My mother-in-law has said she will come over in the mornings to watch Eligh while I take Jonah. Jonah has had a few visits and enjoys playing with children his own age. He has problems with his speech, and so he is allowed to attend full time; the social worker thinks this will encourage his speech to develop. He also attends speech therapy sessions once a week.

In the evenings, I spend my time decorating the new house. I can paint and wallpaper really well, and I like to make the house look good. I always look out for bargains in the DIY stores. Zitty, on the other hand, thinks nothing of punching holes in the doors after a night in the pub. I am trying to make a home, and he destroys it. If I protest, he gets angry and starts on me, so I would rather him punch a hole in the door. The plan to leave once Eligh was born backfired. It is much harder to leave with two children. My father has been suffering with depression for about a year, and Mam has told me that she cannot cope with me and the children as well. She has also said that I'll keep going back anyway, so what's the point? She has said I have made my bed, so I can lie in it.

Zitty is shaming his parents on a regular basis in front of all the neighbours. People have started to notice him banging on the door, trying to climb in through the windows at two in the morning, shouting abuse at me, and screaming for me to "open the fucking door." I pretend to sleep, secretly hoping the ladder will slip and he'll break his neck. I'm not lucky that way at all. His mother is always complaining about his antics – how can she slag off all the neighbours now? I think, *You raised him, you horrible bitch!* But out loud I simply nod and sympathise. I have learned to keep my mouth shut.

Three months later, I discover that I am pregnant again. It isn't planned, but Zitty's happy because he knows it is tying me to him. Lorna visits now and then; she is busy having fun and has settled down with a bloke who is a few years older than her. She works down the local pub in the evenings, and that is how they met. She has started driving lessons and has put in for her test. She gets on with Zitty, but she can see that he's a loser. Everyone down the pub knows he's a knob, and she often catches him chatting up other women. He's scared of Lorna's new fella, and so he doesn't give her any lip.

I am nineteen weeks pregnant and due to go for my scan. I'm not very big on this baby and have had problems with some spotting. My father-in-law has told Zitty that he can borrow the works van to take me to my appointment. Zitty is pissed off because now he has no excuse and has to come with me. He shows off and demands that I go get him some fags on the way. We don't talk. I would have preferred to catch the bus, but pregnancy gives me travel sickness.

We get to the hospital, and I have drunk a lot of water as instructed by the midwife. I am desperate for the toilet but have to hold onto the pint and a half of fluids for the scan to work. This is taking all my concentration, Zitty is constantly moaning in the background. He complains to the receptionist, and she is polite, but I can tell she thinks he's a prat. It's so embarrassing.

Eventually we go in. I lie on the bed as instructed, and the cold jelly is applied. The radiology assistant is checking the baby. She turns the screen towards her while Zitty is trying to look at it. She explains that she is taking some measurements and will need to check something with the doctor. Zitty asks what's going on. I tell him, "I don't know. It probably doesn't have a hand or something." I am trying not to panic because this has never happened before.

A few minutes later, the doctor comes into the room and introduces himself. He sits in the radiographer's chair and checks the baby's measurements. He tells her she was right to get a second opinion. He asks me to wipe the gel off my belly, and once I have emptied my bladder, we should meet him in the next room. I get up, bewildered, and we do as he says. Zitty is still moaning because time is ticking on.

The doctor and radiographer enter the room, and he tells us that unfortunately my baby is incompatible with life. I don't understand. He then tells us that the baby has a form of spifa bifida, called anencephalic. It means that the baby can live in the womb until the pregnancy is full term, but as soon as he is born, he will die in pain within a few hours. He explains that the baby's skull has not completely fused together, leaving the brain exposed. There is nothing they can do.

It finally registers that the baby is going to die. I feel shock and most of all guilt. I didn't want another child, and it's as if I wished this to happen. The doctor explains that I will have to give birth because I am nineteen weeks along. He asks me if I would like to go home tonight and come back in tomorrow. Or I could stay and be started off today. I tell him I'll stay because if I go home, I won't come back. My husband says nothing, and then he asks if he can ring his parents to let them know; he gets up and leaves the room. He tells his parents what is happening, and they have the boys and agree to mind them overnight. He also calls my mother, tells her the news, and asks if she can come see me. When he comes back into the room, he says he has to take the van back to work; it's just his excuse to disappear.

My parents arrive within two hours. Dad still has depression and is driving me mad. He's going on to my mother, asking her if he needs to stay. She tells him to go home because she is staying with me. I am so grateful to have her here; I don't want to go through this alone.

Twelve hours later, I have been given four pesirees, but they are not working. The nurse has explained that she will give me one more, and if this doesn't induce labour, I will have to go to the theatre, where they will insert one high up into my cervix. That will definitely work. Mam leaves the room as I have my fifth pesiree inserted. I am scared and sore, and I think, *Please let this one work.*

Mam tries to comfort me and tells me about when she lost my sister; she had spina bifida, and she said that looking back, it was a blessing because the baby had no quality of life. An hour or so later, the nurse comes in to check on my progress and examines me. When she completes the procedure she asks if I would like to hold the baby when it is born. I tell her I don't know, and she explains that a lot of women always wonder afterwards what the child looked like and imagine it to be a monstrous-looking foetus. She tells me that if I want to see the baby, I can ask the midwife after it is born. This time the pesiree is working, and I can feel contractions, but I also feel numb inside.

After an hour, my water breaks. I feel a lot of pressure in my groin and manage to push out the baby. It doesn't feel like labour; the baby doesn't make any noise and is tiny. My mother is there holding my hand. I start to cry.

The midwife takes the baby and then comes back to clean me up. I tell her I want to see the baby. Thirty minutes later, she comes into the room and hands me my son. I look into his tiny face. He would have looked like Eligh. His skin is translucent, and I cannot see his deformity, only a tiny, perfect, dead child. My mother looks at him. The nurse has left the room. I can feel a strong presence in the room with us. All I can say is, "He's like an angel." I keep repeating those words. I still cannot explain it; it was a surreal feeling. I knew an angel was in that room with us, waiting to take my son away. I named him Dillon.

Zitty picked me up from hospital the next day. We didn't talk; he drove, and I stared out of the window. All I could see were pregnant women. Before I left the hospital, I asked the nurse if I could have the baby blessed, because I'm Catholic and want to know he will go to heaven. The registrar at the hospital comes to speak to me and says that the baby would have to have been twenty-two weeks old to be buried. After seeing my face crumple, he then tells me rules were made to be broken, and he will arrange a funeral for my son. I have never been so grateful to any man, and I thank him with all my heart. Dillon first has to go for an autopsy. He has to go be examined to determine how this happened and the chances of it happening to me again.

Two weeks later, I bury my son. I insist on just my mother coming to the funeral; Dad is hard work, and I couldn't cope with him at the moment. I later have to include my mother-in-law to keep the peace. To my surprise, Zitty also attends. He couldn't look bad in front of the neighbours – his mother wouldn't have that.

The hospital arranged for a counsellor to visit me at home after my bereavement. Zitty was pissed about that and said I should "get over it". If people told him they were sorry for his loss, he just replied, "She lost it, not me." I had an infection soon after giving birth and was readmitted back into hospital for a D and C. My mother-in-law offered to mind the boys, and I was grateful. I saw the counsellor a few times, but I always had the boys with me, and I couldn't cry in front of them. If I did, they would cry as well because it scared them. So I held it all in, and when they went to bed, I'd run a bath, sit there, and sob my heart out. I grieved alone.

Mam was a good listener, and now we had something in common. She told me that time was a great healer. I told her if I died young, she had to make sure that I was buried with Dillon. My way of coping with my loss was to have another baby. I thought if I could get the baby back, I'd be OK. Four months later, I was pregnant again. This time I was thrilled because it was what I wanted. Zitty wasn't bothered; he had always wanted a girl and so was hoping for a change of sex, but I wanted my boy back. The doctors had told me that there was a 25 per cent chance of having another spina bifida child. I had been advised to take folic acid tablets before conceiving. This was a new recommendation for all woman wanting to start a family.

It was approaching my nineteen-week scan, and I had to go to a hospital in the city for a deep bone scan, to check the baby's spine. I was so nervous, but my mother came with me. I entered the radiographer's room and was told to lie on the bed. She put the cold jelly on my stomach. The scan took longer than normal, and eventually I was allowed to look at the screen. Everything was fine, and she asked if I wanted to know the sex before revealing that I was carrying a healthy baby boy.

Time passed quickly. I made sure I eat a healthy diet throughout the pregnancy. In July I gave birth to a bouncing baby boy with a mop of black hair. I called him Frankie, and he weighed in at a healthy nine pounds, two ounces.

Frankie is such a pleasant, placid baby. I put him down awake, and he lies there until he falls asleep. My mother-in-law is smitten with him and asks to take him for a walk to the local shop most evenings. This is also an excuse because the buggy helps her to carry her daily order of six flagons of Strongbow home. She has been having problems with her shoulder of late, probably due to her daily trips to the shops for supplies. Everyone comments on Frankie's mop of black hair; he looks like Mowgli from *The Jungle Book*. People stop when I am shopping and comment, "Oh, what a beautiful baby girl!! I dress him in pale blue, and he has boy features, but as soon as they see the hair, they look past all that and assume he is a girl. Friends and family comment, "Oh, never mind – another boy." I am thrilled he is healthy. My family is complete.

It is hard getting into a routine with three children under five. Jonah regularly asks me when I am having the next one. I reply, "That's it. I do not want any more." Although his speech had improved, he is now in reception class. Jonah is a nervous child. Every painting he brings home is a black page. If I ask him what it is, and he tells me it is a door. My mother says he has been watching a programme on TV about children, and this is a sign of depression in children.

Jonah is given a book to read each week. I read him the story each night and ask him to repeat the words. He finds it hard to do this. It is frustrating, because he is a bright child and I don't understand it. A few days later, I have to go into town. My mother offers to sit with the children. As I wait for the bus, I notice a lady standing next to me. I see the bus is approaching, and I turn to look at her and smile politely. The lady looks at me and says, "You live in a house full of tears. You will move from that house, but it will get worse before it gets better." I don't reply and get on the bus.

Later, when I got home, I tell my mother what the lady said. Mam replies, "She must have been a gypsy."

I say, "I have only just moved and am never moving again!"

Frankie is four months old and is growing quickly. He is in nine- to twelve-month clothes already. I have been feeling a little sickly of late. I am breastfeeding the baby, and the doctor has put me on the mini pill. I am told to take it the same time every day. I remind her that having three small children means I don't do anything at the same time every day. She recommends that I change my contraception to an injection. As I go into the surgery and see the nurse, I tell her that I haven't had a proper monthly since Frankie was born. She tells me this is because I am breastfeeding, and there is nothing to worry about. She does a pregnancy test to rule it out. It's negative, and I have the injection as planned. Sex is practically non-existent anyway, but I don't want to take any chances.

A month later, I am feeling exhausted all the time. I put it down to running around after three children all day, washing and ironing, and cleaning the house. Two months later, I am due to go for my next injection. When the day of my appointment arrives, I tell the nurse about being so tired, and I explain to her that my stomach is swollen and that I don't feel right. She asks the doctor to examine me. The doctor tells me to put in a water sample. I have to call in for the results the next day. When I get to the surgery, I am nervous and have convinced myself that I am not pregnant. The test result comes back positive. I cannot believe it. I cannot remember when I even slept with Zitty last. A scan is booked.

A week later, I am told I am fifteen weeks pregnant. I also have to go for a special scan. This is with a heart specialist, so they can check the baby doesn't have a hole in the heart due to the contraceptive injection. The doctor explains that I must have been a few weeks pregnant before I had the injection. I am still in shock. I thought my family was complete. I am pregnant for the fifth time in seven years, and I am due to give birth in four and a half months. I ask the midwife about being sterilised after the baby is born. She writes it in my notes and tells me to discuss it with the doctor at the hospital, when I go for my antenatal appointments there. This means that it will be in my notes, and if I have to have an emergency caesarean section, they will sterilise me at the same time. I am twenty-four years old.

While I am at home carrying our child, Zitty acts like a single man. He goes out every weekend and gets into fights. The police have had enough of his behaviour, and after he attends court yet again, he is sentenced to four and a half months in prison. He tries to play on the fact that I am pregnant and asks if I will go to court. I tell him I am too busy and have no one to have the children. I am really thinking, *Like fuck, you prick.* I pray he will go down. This time my wish is granted, and I thank the Lord. At least I know where he is for the remainder of my pregnancy, and I have peace and quiet. It is heaven!

In the time he is in prison, I manage to move house. I do a swap with a couple who had split up and got back together.

The wife only went back on the condition that they would move. The house is run-down and has a coal fire, but it is bigger than my old house, and I can see the potential here. With a lot of TLC, it will be lovely. It is also farther away from the in-laws. I know that it is essential to move away from the nosey parkers if I am ever going to leave Zitty and get a life of my own. Life is bliss with him inside, and I realise I can bring up the kids much easier on my own. I have enough money to buy new bedding for the cot, and I've kitted out the boys with new clothes. Zitty agrees to the move after I tell him it means that his parents will not be able to keep such a close eye on him. I move with the help of my family. His parents babysit for me while I decorate the boys' bedroom. By the time he gets out of prison, I have moved and decorated most of the house. Five weeks later, I give birth to a daughter. Zitty insists that he names her. She is born a healthy seven pounds, four ounces and is named Polly.

I have a natural birth, my quickest: she is born in eight hours. She is the icing on the cake. I have a daughter and love her instantly, but I also know I don't want any more. When she is twelve weeks old, I have my appointment to go into hospital to be sterilised. My mother comments that Zitty should be the one going in for the snip, saying I have been through enough. I ask her to be quiet because I want to have it done. I don't want any more children by anyone. My mind is made up: I am not staying with Zitty for the rest of my life. I am sterilised thirteen weeks later.

Zitty has started staying out all the time. We live separate lives. The less I see of him, the better. The children and I only relax when he leaves the house. He has started hanging around with a rough crowd; they are his new drinking butties. I don't know who they are, and I don't care what he does. My only priority is my children. I am too tired after caring for them and cleaning the house to think about anything else.

I get up one morning and notice bags of rubbish by the back door. It is bin day, so I put them out with the rest of the garbage. Zitty rises from bed around midday, which is normal, and asks me where the bags are. I tell him I have thrown them out for the rubbish man. I do all the household chores, so I don't know what the problem is. He is furious and says it was knock-off gear. The boys who own it are going kill him. He calls me a fucking fat slut, slaps me, and leaves the house. As far as I am concerned, it is a win-win situation. I hope they do it soon because I hate the prick. He goes out most nights, and when he is at home, he makes the children nervous. He is always ill-tempered and screams at them. I am worn out by looking after four children. The physical and mental abuse is also taking a toll on me.

Most nights are the same. I get up to feed Polly, but tonight Frankie is ill and also needs me. Zitty refuses to hold Polly while I get up to see Frankie. I have been up all night and am exhausted. The alarm goes off, and it's a school day, so it's time to sort out the boys. I go into the bedroom and carry the little ones with me. The boys are making some noise, and Zitty starts shouting at them, "Shut the fuck up!"

I snap. I put Frankie and Polly on Eligh's bed, storm into the bedroom, and scream at him to fuck off. I tell him, "They are children. It's their home, and they are only playing. If you don't like it, you can fuck off, because you're nothing but a selfish twat." I walk back into the bedroom and am so proud of myself. I stood up to him, and it worked.

As I start to undress Frankie on the bed, Zitty storms into the bedroom in a rage. He grabs me by my hair and smashes my head against the bunk beds several times. I look at Jonah and put my hand up to tell him not to come near me. Zitty screams at me, "You fucking slut! Don't you ever talk to me like that again, or I'll fucking kill you!" He spits in my face and then storms out of the room.

It's quiet, and the kids are terrified. I wipe the spit from my face, and silent tears run from my eyes. Jonah and Eligh rush to me and ask if I am OK. I have never felt so helpless and humiliated.
I look at them both and reply, "I promise you one day, I will set us free."

After that day, I remain silent. I do not answer back for fear of the children getting hurt as well. Zitty's mood swings continue to get worse. He keeps reminding me that those men whose knock-off items I binned are going to kill him. I think, *If only,* but say nothing. He also tells me that they will beat up me and the kids as well, to get back at him. He makes sure he goes out every night to avoid them. I am left to defend us all if they knock on the door. I don't know who they are. He is a gutless bastard.

A week later, Frankie has an ear infection, and I manage to get an emergency appointment at the doctor's. I leave Polly at my parents and take him down. The boys are in school. Doctor James has been my doctor for years and asks me how I am. It's the first time in a long time anyone has asked me this. She says that she was talking to my mother-in-law, who has spoken about me. I tell her about my terrible marriage and how my husband lives like a single man whilst I struggle to bring up the kids. I tell her about the kids and I being afraid of him, and how although he works, he spends every penny on himself.

Doctor James listens and then replies, "That doesn't sound like a marriage, but a prison sentence." I tell her that I feel like I am in this big hole and will never be able to dig myself out. She suggests a good solicitor might help. I thank her for her advice.

When I leave the surgery, I walk to the phone box. I look for the yellow pages and find the names of local solicitors. I dial the first number and ask to book an appointment to see someone about getting a divorce. I am shaking. The man on the other end of the phone introduces himself as David, and he tells me not to worry.

He books an appointment for the following week and tells me if I don't turn up, he will understand. I put down the phone and feel sick. If Zitty finds out, he is going to kill me. I then realise I'm not really living anyway. I am doing this for my children, and for Dr James. She believes in me, and this gives me the courage to carry on. I attend the appointment the following week.

David introduces himself and shakes my hand. He can tell how nervous I am and reassures me that this meeting is confidential. He asks me if I am married, and when I tell him that I am, he replies, "All right, that makes it slightly more difficult." He explains that if I wasn't married, it would be much easier. He gives me forms to fill out to apply for legal aid, and he tells me to write down some examples of the physical and mental abuse. I write three pages and give it to him the following week. He tells me this will help my case. I tell David that my husband cannot find out about this until it is nearly over, because he will kill me. David asks if I do his washing and ironing, and I reply that I do. I tell him that I do not have marital relations (sex with him) anymore, though this is true.

I have continued to attend my appointments, and David explains the procedures. I have to go to the housing officer and try to get Zitty's name off the lease of the house, or I may lose it. He explains possession is nine-tenths of the law. If Zitty refuses to leave, and his name is on the lease, I will lose my home. I visit the housing officer and have all the kids with me. I explain my situation, and he tells me he cannot take the name off without Zitty's consent. He suggests writing to him. At that point, I freak out and tell him, "No way – he will kill me!" I also ask him how am I going to carry four kids out of the house to safety when he explodes. Zitty has been threatening to stab me for weeks, and I am scared. He knows I am up to something, but he doesn't know what. The housing officer apologises for not being able to help me and tells me there is nothing he can do. Before I get up to leave, I tell him, "It's not being beat up that I am scared of. It's the stress of not knowing when it is going to happen, and how am I going to protect my kids."

I am scared most days now. Zitty keeps asking me what's wrong, and I tell him nothing. I have really bad constipation, and I am in so much pain; the stomach cramps are the worst. Eventually, I manage to go to the toilet, and I feel like I have given birth. I get up early the next day and go shopping with Mam. She knows about the divorce and tells me that he has the right to know. She doesn't know the half of it.

He has told me to bring him fish and chips, and I do as I am told. When I get home, I give him his food. He gets up to look for the vinegar, and he starts knocking everything over in the cupboard and screams in my face, "You are a stupid slut. Where is the fucking vinegar? Who can eat fish and chips without vinegar?" The window is open, and my nosey neighbour can hear everything. I decide now is the time, so I tell him I want a divorce. He just looks at me, and I smile nervously, but I am shaking inside.

I tell him I don't love him, and I want him to leave. He starts screaming that he will have to pay child support, and I tell him I don't want anything from him. He turns into Mr Nice Guy and starts to cry. They are crocodile tears. He begs me not to leave him and tries to hug me, which makes me cringe. I don't back down because I have no intention of changing my mind. When Mr Nice Guy doesn't work, he gets nasty again. I know the routine, and this goes on for two hours. If he's not careful, he'll be late for the pub! Eventually, I lie that I will stop the divorce just to end his tantrums. I have no intention of doing so; I simply want a quiet night because I am wrecked. He leaves for the pub, and I sit down, relieved. I wish my mother would butt out from now on. I'm doing it my way.

The following week, I ring David, and he tells me that the solicitor will be knocking on the door with the divorce papers Saturday or Sunday. He tells me that Zitty has to receive them himself, or it will not work. I thank him and put down the phone. I can't stop shaking.

It's Friday night, and Jonah and Eligh are going for their weekly sleepover at my in-law's. She has the older children because they are easier. Jonah is begging her to take Frankie as well, telling her he will look after him all night. She says she cannot cope with all three. Jonah refuses to leave without him and tells her he will be really good. Eventually she agrees, and I'm amazed. This will make the morning much easier for me. It's as if Jonah knows what is going on. I wave them off and sit down. Zitty has gone to his local. Lorna rings me and asks me how I am. I tell her that I feel like I am being set free, like a bird getting out of a cage. She wishes me luck.

Polly is in bed, so it's time to start preparing. I hide all the knives – he's been threatening to stab me for a while, and I'm not making it easy for him. I have thought of the worst-case scenario. As long as he doesn't stab me in any vital organs, I should be able to survive, because I'm strong and healthy. I know he doesn't want me, but he doesn't want anyone else to have me. I have to get Polly's buggy stacked full of nappies, baby food, and clothes in case I can't get back to the house. If I can't get him to leave the house, he can keep it. It is my home, but I don't care about that – it's only bricks and mortar. My main concern is having a roof over my and the children's heads. The most important things are to me and the kids; everything else can be replaced.

I have an early night and try to sleep, but it evades me. He comes in about 12.30, after chatting to a woman on the phone for over an hour in the phone box outside. We have a house phone, but the twat is so obvious. Good luck to her – she is welcome to him.

Polly stirs at 7.30, I get up quickly to bathe and feed her. Then I settle her into her buggy. I am ready to run. I am a nervous wreck and can't stop shaking. If the solicitor doesn't arrive today, I'll have to leave anyway; I cannot do this any longer. I swear that the angels are looking down on me that day.

As I sit waiting for the door to knock, the phone rings: it is my mother-in-law. She tells me that Eligh has been ill; he has had stomach cramps and has been sick. I ring the doctor and manage to get an emergency appointment. I shout up the stairs, telling him I have to get Eligh, and he just groans. I rush down with Polly to pick him up.

As I get there, she passes the phone to me, telling me it's Zitty. He is pretending to cry and says, "You've got what you wanted."

I think, *Thank fuck for that!* I answer yes and hang up the phone.

I get to the doctor after dropping off the other three at my mother's. I am in there with Dr James, and she is checking Eligh's tummy. Zitty bursts through the door and sits down. I am nervous but know he won't do anything outside the house – he is gutless, Dr James acts very professional and carries on with the examination. She tells me it is a stomach bug, but I should keep an eye on him and bring him back if the symptoms persist.

As we leave the surgery, my mother-in-law is walking towards us. She calls her son and tells him to go with her; after a little persuasion, he agrees. I race back to Mam's. It's over. I'm free. Mam confesses that she didn't think it would be that easy and was worried sick. I don't know whether he will return to the house, so I decide to tell the kids on the way home.

I start by telling Jonah and Eligh that I have some important news. Frankie and Polly are too young to understand. The older two both look at me, nervous. I say, "Your dad's gone. I've thrown him out of our lives."

I hear "Hooray!" and "We might lose the house and have to live somewhere else". Then they give more hoorays. We were all free!

New Beginnings

Zitty went back to live with his mother that day. Possession is nine-tenths of the law, which means the children and I get to stay in the house. I ring an emergency number and have the locks changed on the house the day he left. I make sure the doors and windows are locked day and night, in case he tries to come into the house. If I see him outside, I ignore him. He is gutless, and I know he cannot hurt me or the children outside of these four walls. I get an injunction against him. My dad takes me to the courthouse, and Zitty storms into the waiting room and ignores my solicitor (who tries to introduce himself). We have to wait thirty minutes before entering the courtroom. I can feel Zitty's eyes burning into me; he is furious. It is the longest thirty minutes of my life, but I refuse to look at him.

We are called into court, and he pushes past everyone and smashes the door against the wall on the way in. The judge tells him to calm down, or he will have him removed. This works in my favour; my dad sees Zitty's true colours for the first time. I am awarded my injunction.

My former mother-in-law rings and asks for some furniture and his clothes to be dropped off at her house. I reluctantly give him a spare set of drawers. It's a bedside cabinet that I bought; he never contributed anything to the house. I bagged up his clothes. She also wanted back my engagement ring.

Dad dropped off all the items. When he came back, he told me that he had been chatting to her, and although she admitted the breakup was 70 per cent his fault, my 30 per cent was much worse. She also added, "He is a nice-looking lad and will have no problem finding someone else," whereas I had four children, so who else would want me?

My reply to my dad was, "Yep, I do have four beautiful children, and I do not want anyone else after being married to that knobhead for seven years!" I decide that is his new nickname, Knobhead.

The divorce is completed within three months. I qualified for legal aid. My former mother in-law rings me every few weeks to inform me that Knobhead wants to speak to me about the children. l agree to speak to him. His first words are, "Why are you doing this to me?" I hang up. We have agreed that the children can visit Knobhead and his parents for three hours after school on Wednesdays and Fridays. When she arrives to pick them up, he is not allowed near the house. She comments that she found a pair of women's knickers in his room the other day. I tell her they are not mine and wish him luck. The news does not have the desired effect.

A few days later, I am awoken suddenly in the middle of the night. I have left my top bedroom window open and can hear someone calling my name. I'm terrified because it's him, and he is trying the door handle. I know it is locked.

I creep down the stairs, ducking past the windows. The phone is at the bottom of the stairs, and he is walking around the side of the house. I pick up the phone and ring his parents. His mother answers the phone. I ask if he has come home yet; it's about 1.30 in the morning. She replies that he hasn't, so I tell her he is outside my house, and if she and her husband don't come and get him within the next ten minutes, I'm ringing the police. She knows that I mean it.

I can hear him trying the back door, and so I sit by the phone, feeling sick. Five minutes later, I can hear his parents calling his name and asking him to go home with them. He is drunk and crying, saying, "Why is she doing this to me?" Relief washes over me. I recheck all the windows and doors before going to bed.

After that night, he gets the message, and things settle down. His mother hates me, the main reason being because I hurt her little bastard. The other reason is because she now has to deal with him and his moods, and she doesn't want the spoilt brat back. Luckily for her, within six months he moves in with the owner of the mysterious knickers. I am glad she has done me a favour.

For the first time in my life, I am truly free to make my own decisions. I am twenty-four years old and divorced with four children. My parents cannot tell me what to do anymore. Living on my own with my children is my only option. The months pass by quickly. The children are improving in school, and Jonah's reading has improved overnight. His teacher rings me at home and asks me to call into the school. He is given an award, and she cannot get over the improvement. It is as if the stress has lifted off us all, and we are happy. My parents are a great help. Dad has recovered from his depression and helps me ferry the children to and from school. Mam babysits for me to go out once a fortnight. I have started to make friends, and for the first time in years, I can hold my head up high and speak to people without being afraid of the consequences.

I take the children swimming on the weekends, and we go to the park. I do not have time restrictions. It doesn't matter if we are home an hour late. My former mother in-law's version of this is that I am always out on the road, dragging the children behind me! She tells anyone who will listen. She is a bitch and is not well liked. My neighbours confide in me, now that I am divorced, that she has been nicknamed "the poison dwarf" for years. Her height is four foot nothing!

I have been thinking about my future. What do I want to do? I decide to enrol in the local college because I am interested in a hairdressing course. They are holding an open evening in a month, and my mother has agreed to watch the children for me to attend. I decide to enrol on a hairdressing NVQ level two fast-track course for young mothers.

The course is run during school hours. Frankie will qualify for a full-time nursery place, and I have secured a place in the college creche for Polly. Jonah is starting junior school, and Eligh will attend the second year of infants in September. My mother has been a rock since my divorce and is happy about me attending college. She cannot do her own hair and has offered to be a model whenever I need one.

Sophie is pregnant with her first child. She had her dream wedding last year, and she married within a year of meeting her husband. She has asked if I would like to mind my new nephew or niece for her to go back to work. I refuse because I am set on going to college. It is time for me to get some qualifications and a career.

Lorna is living with her boyfriend, the one she met in the pub. She has a new puppy that is very cute, a Yorkshire terrier, named Poppy.

Andy has married his long-term girlfriend, Sammy. They haven't been lucky enough to conceive yet, but they are trying for a baby. Sammy is blaming Andy. He has been banned from wearing his favourite Wrangler Texas jeans, and he needs to keep his plums cool, so he has to wear jogging bottoms or shorts. They have gone to the fertility clinic, and this was the verdict. I wonder whether the fact that she drinks in the club every night whilst Andy babysits her sister's kids has any effect. I shut my mouth but secretly wish he would wise up. His mates are always telling him he's henpecked, and I'm inclined to agree.

It is six months since my divorce has been finalised, and I am due to start my college course in September. I have discovered that I qualify for a grant, and this has enabled me to buy my uniform and my hairdressing kit. I get income support and am coping much better on my own. I ask my family to buy the children's clothes instead of loads of toys for birthdays and Christmas. This helps out a lot. I work out my income and outgoings to the last penny, and I have lists months in advance. This means I know how much money I have left for things like Christmas presents for the children. Mam has a catalogue, and I pay weekly for presents. I am very organised and don't waste a penny. I have set goals, a list of things I want to achieve within the next five years. First, I want to pass my hairdressing level two course, and then I want to go on to hairdressing level three and achieve that. They are both fast-track courses, and I will achieve them in two years. Next, I want to get a part-time job in a hair salon. Finally, I want to pass my driving test and get a car. I am twenty-five and have given myself until I am thirty to achieve these goals.

My parents have suggested that the children should have a holiday, and they offer to book a Chateau at a Butlins Resort. Dad has told me they will pay for the week's stay and provide the transport. Mam says that it will do us the world of good. Sophie has agreed to come with me; she is seven months pregnant. It is booked for a month's time.

A week before the holiday, Sophie goes into labour early and gives birth to a tiny boy; he weighs four pounds, thirteen ounces and has to stay in intensive care. She names him

George. I tell my new friend Gemma about the baby and the holiday, and she offers to take her place. She has three sons who are friends with my boys and are the same age. Gemma rings the resort and changes the booking. Her boyfriend works a lot and doesn't mind her going. He doesn't have time to go away with them and tells me it will do them good. He has arranged a day off work to take them, and we will meet them there. The children are thrilled.

Gemma is better off than me and has a lot more spending money for the holiday. I manage to save about 150 pounds at short notice and will have to cash in my family allowance while I am there.

The day we are due to leave, Jonah is ill, and I have to take him to the doctor. He has tonsillitis and is given antibiotics and Calpol for his temperature. Jonah sleeps the whole way there and is really ill. I leave him with my dad in the car while we unpack. I have taken my own pillows and bedding; it's like we are moving house. I carry Jonah into the chaleau and put him onto the bed. There are seven children and two adults, and the children cannot wait to start having fun.

We manage to get the children to the pool area. I have dosed up Jonah and carry him there. Gemma has helped to push Polly in her buggy. Jonah is worried that his new friend is angry because he is too ill to go into the pool, and he constantly asks him, "Are you still my friend?"

The boy replies, "Yes, but only if you stop asking me!"

Jonah has repeated it at least fifty times. I give him a hug and try to reassure him. I tell him there is no need to keep asking him; the boy is his friend, and he knows that he cannot help being ill. Jonah is so afraid of losing him. He is only eight years of age and is a bag of nerves; this is what living with Knobhead has done to him.

Within three days, the antibiotics are working, and Jonah is playing with his new friend and having fun, though he is still asking him if he is still his friend every five minutes. Gemma doesn't understand, but I constantly reassure Jonah and give him loads of hugs. Inside, I could cry for him.

Eligh is five, and nothing is too hot or heavy for him. I watch him whizzing down the thirty-foot slide backwards, forwards, and on his side. He has a massive smile on his face as he runs towards the ladder for another go. Jonah is too nervous to go on there; Frankie and Polly paddle in the pool. Tomorrow we are going to the beach, and the last day we are going to the funfair. I have managed to stretch out the cash by making the children share chips and pop. I manage with a chip roll. The plus side of this is I have lost nearly two stone since the divorce, and I am back in my size ten jeans.

Chapter

It is six months since the holiday. Gemma and I have become good friends, and we have a night out once a fortnight. Mam will only babysit every two weeks, and the kids love it. It is the first time I have gone out and been single; although I have four children, I have only ever slept with Knobhead. Gemma tells me I have been single long enough, and if it was her, she would be on the pill. I am so naive that I don't even know when a man is chatting me up or just talking to me. I have no confidence.

Gemma tells me that men look at me all the time when we are out, but I never notice. She spots her boyfriend's cousin, who is younger than me. I know him from school. She has a word with him and gets him to buy us both a drink. She tells me that he is interested in me and that I should see him tonight. She reminds me that Knobhead is with someone else, and I need to have some fun. We are both drunk, and so I agree. Gemma arranges for him to stay at her house until my mother leaves. I get in and see my mother into the taxi. I then ring her house, and she tells me he is walking up. Gemma and I live about two hundred yards from each other. She giggles and wishes me luck, reminding me that she wants all the details tomorrow. I agree to her demands and put down the phone. I quickly check on the kids, who are all asleep.

Ten minutes later, there is a knock at the door.

I am so nervous but let him in; the drink has given me confidence. We chat about people from school for a while, and then he asks if we should head on up to bed. He follows me up the stairs. I insist on leaving the light off, and we clumsily undress. He asks if I am on the pill, and I tell him I'm sterilised. I am under the covers as soon as my clothes hit the floor. He takes the lead and starts to kiss me, I respond, and soon we are having sex all night. This bloke must have taken a Viagra or something!

We chat a bit in the morning, I am conscious of the time. It is six o'clock, and I want him up and gone by the time the kids wake up.

He leaves at six thirty, and I am relieved, I lock the door and go back to bed. At ten thirty the phone is ringing. It's Gemma, wanting all the gossip. My head is still throbbing, but I tell her all the details.

Gemma and I go out a fortnight later, and he is in the pub, sat with his mates. They are looking at me with smirks on their faces. I am gutted that he has told everyone. This is my worst nightmare. Everyone thinks I am a slapper! I tell Gemma that I am never speaking to him again. She apologises and says she didn't know he was like that. I reply, "He's a fucking man, isn't he?" That is my worst date ever.

It is our first Christmas without Knobhead. I am looking forward to it but have set rules. The routine used to be that both sets of grandparents would turn up about ten thirty. I have informed Knobhead and his parents that I will drop them off about eleven thirty and pick them up before dinner, so that they can see them and give them their presents.

My mother thinks I am being hard. I politely tell her to butt out, because I have them all year, and Christmas is my day. Knobhead and his parents are no longer welcome in my house. I will not have an atmosphere on Christmas Day anymore. Knobhead hardly sees the children and has no interest in them. He prefers Eligh and Polly and shows it, whereas his mother favours Jonah and Frankie (Jonah because he is the firstborn, and she thinks he looks the most like Knobhead; Frankie because he is an angel and is such a placid child). This behaviour infuriates me. I treat them all the same, and they have the same amount spent on them to the nearest penny.

On Christmas Eve, my favourite day of the year, the children are bathed and go to bed early. They ask if they can, so I let them because I have loads to do! The boys watch television in their room, and Polly is asleep. I clean the house from top to bottom and do all the washing and ironing. Next, I make pasties and put the meat in to cook. I make the stuffing, do all the dishes, and clean the kitchen afterwards. We are going for dinner at my parents', but I like to have meat and stuffing for Boxing Day. Later, I put out the Quality Street and presents. The children are fast asleep, and I check them and tuck them in. They look so peaceful and contented. Finally, I pour myself a glass of wine and run a hot bubble bath. I sink in the warm, soapy water and soak my aching body. I am shattered; it is two thirty in the morning. I get into bed around three thirty and shut my eyes for what feels like five seconds.

Suddenly, I am being shaken awake by Jonah and Eligh. Frankie and Polly are bouncing on the bed, and they are all shouting, "Has he been? Has he been?"

I reply, "Yes, I think he has!" I am still shattered, but we get up and go downstairs. I tell them whose presents are for whom, and within ten minutes there is wrapping paper everywhere. This is the best Christmas ever!

My parents arrive later with gifts. For the first time ever, we can enjoy Christmas without any atmosphere, and everyone is welcome in my house. Lorna and I drop off the children for their visit. Knobhead's mother is worried that I have time to enjoy myself – so we head to the pub for an hour just to piss her off! All the locals have arrived in their new jumpers, scarves, socks, and coats. Lorna's other half is in the pub with his mates. We have a chat and two halves of Strongbow, and then we head to pick up the kids after dropping off their gifts at the house. Poundstretcher did well this year! We all head to Mam's for Chrimbo dinner.

It is nearly June 1997, and I have completed the first year of college and my level two NVQ in hairdressing. I am so chuffed; my mother has had four perms, nine colours, and fifteen haircuts this year. She's a star! Gemma has been a model for me as well. Lorna comments that kids fringes are getting much straighter. I have enrolled in my level three NVQ course for next term. Polly will go to nursery full-time, and Frankie is starting reception class in school. The nursery teacher asks if Polly is like her brother, commenting that she hasn't heard him talk all year. I reply, "No, you will know you have her!" She bosses him around a lot and is very independent, even though she is only three. Lorna has a soft spot for her. Sophie is pregnant again and is hoping for a daughter this time.

Sophie asks me if I would like to visit a fortune teller with her. She has gone for years and tells me that she knows of a lady who is very good. I am curious and wonder what she will predict, so we book it for the following week. Mam offers to mind the children.

I am nervous as we go into the ladies home. Sophie tells me I can go in first because she has been loads of times. I am led into the lady's kitchen. She tells me to sit down and gives me a crystal ball to hold. She tells me to hold it in my hands for a few minutes before wrapping it in a cloth and taking it from me. She then looks into the palm of my hands and tells me I have had five children, although she only sees four now. She says that I won't have any more. She looks further, predicts a long life, and shows me my lifeline. She tells me that I will not be stabbed or killed by anyone. She then tells me that she can see a bingo or lottery win around me, and a person will take me and my children on a holiday. She explains that it will be OK, but not great, and that we will travel on a water taxi boat to the main island.

She tells me that one of my four children will go far in life, and one will go into the forces. She also says that one day I will go far overseas and have more money than I will know what to do with. I ask her if I will go there to visit the child who is going to do really well. She tells me, "No, you will go for yourself." She tells me details about my parents and friends, and whom to trust and not to trust. She says that there is a false friend around me who cannot be trusted, so I should be aware of her. There are several people like that on my college course so that makes sense. She tells me that I will not meet a man for several years; there is someone there for me, but he is in a bad relationship at the moment and will not break free from it until later. I thank her and leave, giving Sophie her turn before heading home. The lady predicts that Sophie will have a daughter.

Six months later, it is a Sunday afternoon. We are at my parents', and the kids and I have been swimming. Sunday lunch is ready for us when we get to Mam's. Lorna is usually here by now, and I don't know what is keeping her. She arrives an hour later, white as a ghost and repeating constantly, "Shut up, shut up! I've just won seventy-five thousand pounds on a scratch card!" We all tell her not to be so stupid, but she shows us the card, and there are three seventy-five-thousand-pound figures there. Lorna has won the lottery!

I tell her if she is going to give me anything, all I want is a holiday. The children and I have never been abroad. She is shaking, and we decide to take it to the store that she bought it from to get advice on how to claim the money. After adding her name to the back of the card, the shop assistant tells us that she cannot claim that amount in the store and has to ring the number on the back of the card. She collects her cheque the next day, and a week later she books us a holiday. Lorna, the kids, and I are going to Ibiza!

Two weeks later, Lorna tells me that she has booked her new best friend Mary and our mutual friend Sara to come as well. Her reason for this was she thought that it would lighten the workload, and we could look after one child each. She also tells me that I have to find my own spending money. I tell her that's all right; I will do that, and I'm simply happy to be going abroad for the first time. The holiday is booked for the following August, and I have to get a passport. I am able to put the children's names on mine, and I start saving. I will have finished college by then, so the timing is great.

I have started going out and drinking on a weekly basis. I am doing a bit of mobile hairdressing at home and am able to earn fifteen pounds on top of my income support. This pays for the babysitter; my mother doesn't want to be committed to having the children every fortnight, and she is not happy about my weekly arrangement. Gemma gave me the name of a babysitter named Emma. Emma is very mature for fifteen years of age, and Jonah gets on great with her. I usually go out with Sara, Lorna's friend from work. They went on holidays every year together until Lorna settled down. Gemma joins us about once a month.

Sara and I are both single, and we go out and meet up with Sara's friends. It is nice not to be mam for one night of the week. My hairdressing course is stressful because I have a lot of coursework, along with the housework and seeing to the children. I do all my own decorating. I have to do this when the children are in bed, and I often stay up all night. Then I have to get the kids up and go to college. I don't think my mother understands that I need time out.

I have not had time to date. After the disastrous one-night stand, I decided not to bother. A year has passed since that night, and I have to admit I am feeling lonely. I am not craving mad, passionate sex, but a hug and someone to talk to for an evening would be nice. Sara is very fussy when it comes to men. They have to wear the right clothes, have an earring, and have nice teeth. I am looking for someone who makes me laugh. He does not have to handsome, but I do have to fancy him a little. He needs to like children and be kind. I chat to men who are really nice and like children, but I don't fancy them. I look around and see men who are nice looking but are out of my league. I chat to men who are funny. I decide I need all three qualities or nothing at all.

I have learned that the most precious thing in my life are classified as baggage by everyone else, including my friends and drinking partners. If I chat to man for more than five minutes, Sara or one of her friends feels the need to inform him that I have four children. They do add that I am a nice girl, but am I supposed to be grateful for that? I chat to Lorna about it and tell her that if I want to tell a man about my children, I will. Half the time I don't even fancy the men, so why do they have to warn them? It's embarrassing. I add that I am not ashamed of having children, but it's none of their business. Lorna's advice is to tell Sara; she probably doesn't realise what she is doing. I can't be bothered. We are going on holidays together, and I don't want anything to spoil it.

I have completed my college course, and the children have finished school for the holidays. I have managed to kit out the kids with new clothes, and I've saved up enough spending money to go away. I read through their school reports. Jonah's tells me that he tends to be a daydreamer, and he is very good at art. His grades are slightly above average, and he is meeting all his targets. He is well behaved and polite. I am happy with that.

Next I read Eligh's. He is excellent at art and has won a competition with the local paper for the school this year. His grades are above average, and he is a popular member of the group. He is a polite, friendly child and is a pleasure to teach. Great news!

Frankie is very quiet in class, and he has to have extra one-to-one help with reading, writing, and mathematics. They have referred him for tests for dyslexia.

However, Frankie is a pleasure to teach and will be missed by his teacher next year. Frankie is very shy outside of the house. I tell him that he has done really well, and I explain about the tests and tell him it is nothing to worry about.

Polly's report states her social life is getting in the way of her schoolwork. She is four! She is a bubbly member of the group who likes to organise her peers. The teacher tells me that her work is above average, and she enjoys painting; I have loads of her artwork in the kitchen to prove it. She adds in spite of this, Polly is a polite, friendly child and will be missed next year. I laugh, give Polly a big kiss, and tell her well done.

My bossy little girl tries to rule the roost in the house, but the boys shut their bedroom door in her face. Frankie is always torn; he likes her, but he wants to be one of the boys, and Polly loses out every time.

Eventually, it is the night before the holiday. I have three of them in the bath, and as usual Frankie has run off to hide; this is his ritual! I managed to undress him before he wriggled free. I look in the bedroom but can't see him. Ten minutes later, there is a knock on the door, and I answer it. It is one of the neighbours who lives opposite me, she asks me if I can get my son out of the window. I step outside and look up. There's Frankie, stood on the windowsill behind the curtain and thinking no one can see him! His hairy little bum is against the glass. I thank her for letting me know, go upstairs, and peer behind the curtain.

Frankie says, "Argh! How did you know where I was hiding?" I tell him that the whole street can see him! Jonah and Eligh are hysterical as Frankie's jaw hits the floor. I bathe Frankie and put them all to bed. I tell them to settle down because tomorrow we are going on a plane!

We have a minibus to the airport. My parents come down to wave us off, and Knobhead's parents walk up to see them. Knobhead's stepdad pushes a twenty-pound note into their hands and tells them that ten pounds of it is from them, and ten is from their dad. He also tells, "The money is for you, no one else." He means me, the cheeky twat.

Knobhead's mother pipes up, "Don't forget, kids. Your granddad, your dad, and I want a present off each of you." The tight bitch – she has no chance.

Three months earlier, Knobhead came back from Planet Hollywood in Florida with his new girlfriend. He had photos taken with Arnold Schwarzenegger and Bruce Willis, and he showed the kids. As an afterthought, he gave them a Planet Hollywood snow dome for them to share. He has kept to his word and has not given a penny in maintenance since the divorce. As far as I am concerned, he can stick it up his arse!

As soon as we arrive at the resort and settle in, I take the kids to the local supermarket. I tell them we are getting the requested presents now so that they don't have to worry about it later on. We decide on an ashtray for Nan and a box of fudge for Granddad. Oh, marvellous – a snow dome for Knobhead! We go to the till, and the shop owner tells us that it is three euros. I tell the kids that's their present shopping done, and the rest of the money is for them. Jonah wants to spend all of his straight away, but I tell him to save some for another day. Eligh sees a wrist band he wants. Polly wants a cheap Spanish doll; it's ten euros. Frankie spends one euro and tells me he's saving his. He's his mother's son!

We get back to the apartment and head to the pool. I plaster the kids in sun cream. Sara, Lorna, and Mary are already out on sun loungers, trying to get a good tan. I watch the kids play in the pool, and the next thing I hear is Jonah saying, "Cor! Look at the bristol cities on Sara!" I look over, and she is topless. Eligh and Frankie are giggling. I tell her if she is going to go topless, the boys are going to look. Her bikini top goes back on. Within two hours, I am itching with prickly heat and spend the rest of the holiday in the shade. Lorna has decided that she and Mary will share a room with Jonah and Eligh, and Sara and I will go next door with Frankie and Polly.

The next morning, I wake up to a slapping sound and Sara telling her to go wake her mother up. I look into the next bedroom, and Polly is slapping her on the cheek, constantly calling her name. She is trying to wake her up so that she can get her breakfast.

Next door to our hotel is a bar with entertainment and a bouncy castle slide. Every night the children watch the castle slide inflating and can't wait to go there. We go to the pool most days. We are there for two weeks. I am used to being careful with money and worry that I won't have enough, because we are self-catering. The children ask for lollies, and

I tell Jonah to come with me to the supermarket around the corner. Lorna snaps, "Just get them by the bar, for fuck's sake!" Everyone hears her, and I am so embarrassed. She pushes a twenty-euro note into Jonah's hand and tells him to get one for her. She asks, "Do you want anything?" I reply no and tell her to watch the kids if it's not too much trouble, because I'm going into the pool. I am upset but will not show her. Sometimes she can be a nasty bitch.

Sara wants to go to Manumission on the weekend. It's a nightclub on the island, and apparently a top DJ is playing there on Saturday night. Lorna and Mary have boyfriends and do not want to go. Lorna tells me that if I go with Sara on Saturday, then she and Mary will take the kids out all day and give me chance to get ready for the night. Lorna says that it will give me a break. I agree to go and thank her for offering to have the kids. On Friday evening, Lorna tells me that she and Mary are going to the market on Saturday alone, because if they have to have the kids that night, they are having a break. I have already purchased my ticket, and Sara wants to go nightclubbing.

On Saturday morning, I get up and take the children to the beach. We buy buckets and spades, and they have a great time. Sara stays in the room to get some sleep for that night. Lorna and Mary have gone shopping. The children and I head back to the pool before returning to the room at around six o'clock. Lorna, Mary, and Sara are in the room, and it is full of smoke. Lorna and Mary have constantly chain-smoked since we arrived because the fags are so cheap. Lorna tells me that they are all going for food because they are having the kids tonight. I shower, change, and feed them all. It is ten o'clock before they get back. Sara is raring to go, so I have a bite to eat and get ready. We leave for the nightclub, but all I really want to do is go to bed! We head out to the bay and manage to catch the last water taxi to the island.

It takes us two hours to get to the there, and we arrive at Cafe Mamba first. It has emptied out, and the taxis and buses are packed. An hour later, we manage to get a taxi to the club. When we arrive, we are given a complimentary drink voucher to redeem at the bar. It is packed, and there are transvestites dancing on large boxes and people dressed in black crow costumes, walking around. Everyone has a bottle of water and a glow stick. The music is shit, and Sara is telling me to look over at the VIP area because she can see Denise Van Outen. I think, *Whoopee! You can't get anywhere near them anyway, or see the DJ.* I get to the bar and ask for a cider, but they only have larger, which I hate. I get a bottle of water.

I look around the room and see a film playing on a projector screen. A gay man is talking dirty to someone (I am not sure if it is a man or a woman) who is in a dentist's chair. It is the weirdest thing I have ever seen. Sara is loving it, but I am exhausted and think, *Beam me up, Scotty!* I tell her I have to go because I feel dizzy. I know she is pissed off, but I cannot stand it here any longer.

On the way back, we start chatting to some younger lads. They ask us who we are here with, and Sara tells them that we have come with another two adults and my four children. Within seconds I am walking alone, and Sara is still happily chatting away to them. They leave, we bump into another crowd, and it happens again. I don't want to get off with anyone, but they make me feel like a leper! My life is worlds apart from these people, and I can't wait to get back to my kids.

We arrive back at the resort at 5.30 a.m. I manage to have a lie in until 9.00, and then I take the children to the beach. The next day is overcast, so I suggest taking Frankie and Eligh to the water park on the other side of the island. Lorna offers to mind the younger two. We catch the local bus, and I pack some biscuits and drinks. We have the best day going on the slides with no moody adults. When we arrive back, Lorna is moaning that we are late. I ask if the little ones have been good, and she tells me that they have been taking photos of them and admits that they have been no trouble. I shower them and head down to their favourite location. Lorna, Mary, and Sara inform me that they are going off for food together alone because they need a break!

We have two days left of the holiday. The boys are running out of clean underwear, so I decide to just put them in shorts. The children and I head to the bouncy castle bar. Jonah and Eligh have gone into the park area; a lady minds the children, and it is fenced off. They charge two euros per child, but they can go back and forth all night and are safe. I tell them that I am inside with Frankie and Polly. Polly is asleep in the buggy. Eligh has been complaining of a bad stomach, and I have given him an extra dose of his medicine. He takes Senercot and Lacterlose because he has suffered with constipation since he was three years of age. I get the children some pop and order myself a drink because we have eaten in the room.

A crowd has come from outside and taken a table opposite us. I haven't seen them in here before, so I'm guessing that they have just arrived. I relax and take a sip of my drink. As I look up, I see Eligh running towards me holding his bum. He is bouncing up and down and asking me where the toilets are. I direct him to the other side of the entertainment room. It's about thirty metres away, and I tell him to run; I cannot go with him and leave the little ones. He runs across the room, and as he does, he keeps looking back in horror. As I look more carefully, I see small cow pats appearing on the floor. He stops and panics, and I shout, "Run!" He disappears into the toilet.

Eventually, Lorna and the others arrive back. I tell her to watch the little ones before rushing off. An argument is erupting at the next table, and I can hear them saying, "It isn't me!" That's all I need! I pick up several table mats and try to scoop the pats into the nearest bin, using baby wipes to clean the floor. Then I go in to sort out Eligh. He isn't in the ladies, so I call his name and hear a little voice coming out of the gents. I tell him to come out here so that I can clean him up, and he is so embarrassed. I take him into the toilet and do the best job I can. As I am washing his hands, I look up and see the lady from the other table. She has a brand-new white trainer in her hand, and she is trying to wash off Eligh's poo! I look at her and say sorry. I take Eligh back to the room and then shower and change him before heading back to bar. As I enter, the table of people are all staring at me. I say, "Sorry about that." They erupt, laughing hysterically.

Eventually it is time to head back home. We arrive at the airport at about one thirty in the morning. The children are shattered. I can hear Lorna, Mary, and Sara arguing about who is sitting with the kids on the way home. None of them want to. I tell them if I could physically sit with them all, I would, but I can't, so they need to grow up. Lorna's attitude hurts the most because she is my sister, their aunty.

When we get home, my mother is at my house with a cup of tea, waiting for me. She has gone to the shops and got supplies for breakfast. The children go to bed to sleep, and she asks me how it went. I start to cry. I tell her I will never go on holidays with Lorna or anyone else again.

I go out with Sara the following week, and one my drinking partners tells me that Sara has been telling everyone that my kids are little bastards! I tell Sara she can call me what she likes, but she can't call my kids names. Sara denies saying it, and the friendship is over.

Mam has a word with Lorna and tells her how much she has upset me. I get a gift off her, when all I really wanted is for her to say sorry. A month later, Sophie gives birth to a daughter. She is beautiful, and she calls her Liona.

The children start back to school. I have finished my college course and have been applying for part-time work. My mother tells me that she would prefer to mind the children for me, and as long as it is only part-time hours, she can do it around her job. Two weeks later, I get a job in a local hair salon as a stylist. I apply for tax credits, and after working out my money, I am only five pounds a week better off – but I am earning it myself and am independent. Goal number three has been achieved. I book driving lessons, and it takes me over a year, but on my third test I pass. I am so chuffed.

I visit Gemma and tell her my news. she replies, "Well, if you can do it, so can I!" She books a lesson. I cannot afford a car yet; that is my next goal.

Finding Mr Right has had to take a backseat. I have been far too busy to date, but as Christmas approaches, I feel lonely. My house is always busy with the children, and my family and friends are great, but the worst time to be single is Christmas. Gemma decides to help out and sets me up with one of her partner's friends on a night out. We arrange to meet up as a foursome. Gemma and I pre-drink and are drunk before we enter the pub. He is a nice guy, the drinking goggles are on, and I fancy him. The rest of the night is a blur.

The next morning I wake up, and my head and groin are both aching. I suddenly remember my date came home with me. As I turn around, I see a mop of ginger hair on the pillow next to me. No way! I have shagged a glow-in-the-dark! I am going to kill Gemma. I make sure he leaves before the children rise.

The next few weeks are filled with getting the house ready for the festive season.

I spend my days doing housework and seeing to all the children's needs. After school I feed them, bathe them, and put them to bed. Going downstairs should be my time to relax, but this is when the chores such as mowing the lawn, painting the house, and all the DIY jobs are done. The living room needs a coat of paint. I start with the ceilings, and it is a double room with an archway in the middle. I have chosen a light coffee colour for the walls. I cut in the edges and use a paint pad to give the walls three coats of paint. I am listening to the radio and singing to all the old songs. It's times like this that I am glad my neighbour is an alcoholic and is probably too drunk to hear me. I finish the walls, and in between waiting for the coats to dry, I gloss the radiators. The skirting boards are stained, and I finish painting, clean up, and wash out the brushes. I then shower and get into bed at around six thirty.

Jonah shakes me awake at eight thirty, asking me to find his PE kit. I am so tired that I feel like I have been superglued to the mattress. I am aching all over and have used muscles I never thought I had.

My mother arrives at 8.45. This is routine, and she gives me a hand to get them to school. She gives me a row and tells me if I had waited, she would have given me a hand. I peg out the curtains; I have washed them and will put them back up tonight. I look around the room and am proud of my achievement. We drop the children at school, and I head to Mam's for a cuppa and a chat. She tells me that I do not need a man in my life because I am doing fine on my own. I have bags under my eyes and am shattered. She has always had my dad and does not understand. The only people who tell me this are the ones who are attached.

Christmas is days away. The boys have asked for Power Rangers, and I have already bought them and stored them at Mam's. The news is reporting that they are the top present this year, and stocks are running out, so I am glad I got them early. I got Polly a pram and doll, and Frankie wants a Ghostbuster car and men. This is all he has asked for. The boys have also asked for a BMX bike each. I have been paying weekly for them and will pick them up Christmas Eve. Dad has offered to pick them up and store them at his house; he will drop them down for me in the evening, when the boys are asleep. I love to surprise them, and Christmas Day is going to be great!

Work is going well. The shop has several part-time staff and a full-time stylist. The full-timer is younger than me and very bitchy. The manager of the salon often sides with the full-timer for a quiet life, and this creates friction and bad customer service. I go out on a Saturday night every week. I have friends whom I meet through work and from the school.

Dad is dropping me off one week, and he drives past an empty shop near the town. It is a closed clothes shop, but I remember that a few years ago, it was a hair salon. I wonder, *Could I do that? I have an idea.*

I wait until Monday morning, and after dropping the children at school, I visit the college's hairdressing department and ask if my old tutor is available. The receptionist tells me to take a seat because she will be back from lunch in ten minutes. When she enters the salon, she is pleased to see me and asks how I am getting on. I fill her in on my new job and ask her if she can give me some advice. I tell her I have seen an empty shop and was thinking of opening my own salon. I ask her what she thinks. She looks shocked because she knows I have four children, and she asks how I will cope. I tell her I am simply considering it at the moment. She tells me that when she opened her own salon, she bought second-hand equipment, and her children were of school age. She also said that it can be achieved with enough hard work and determination. I ask her how would I go about getting in touch with the owner of the property, and she advised me to go to an estate agent in town.

I thank her and ask her to keep it to herself. She wishes me luck and asks me to keep her updated. I walk to town and ask in every estate agent office. The last one tells me that the lady in the fruit and vegetable shop next door is friendly with the owner. I thank her and leave. I get the number and ring up the owner of the property. She is very friendly and tells me that she is waiting to hear from a beautician within the next three days; she has to give her first refusal. I decide to wait four days. I have drawn a sketch of the shop inside and planned the interior. I have given the shop a name: Lauren's Hair Studio. I have also designed the window sign. Three days pass, and I cannot wait any longer. I ring the landlady back.

She tells me to ring back this afternoon. If she hasn't heard from the beautician, I can view the property.

I am a bag of nerves because I want this so badly that it hurts. I ring back at two o'clock. She tells me the beautician hasn't come back to her, so we arrange a time to view the property. She also adds that she told her husband she was hoping that the beautician wouldn't, because she could tell I was so desperate to get the property. If she had to deliver bad news, she was afraid I might hang myself! I tell her I really want to do this. I have never been more determined in my whole life!

I ask Dad to come with me and not to tell Mam just yet. I explain that I am thinking of opening my own salon. He tells me that he has never lied to her before, but he agrees to come along. As I look around, the landlady tells me the cost of the rent, water rates, and business rates on the building. I look around: it needs a lick of paint and some DIY on the place, but other than that, it is perfect. She agrees to give me six weeks' free rent to allow me time to redecorate and open for business. She also tells me she knows of a place that sells second-hand hairdressing equipment, and she will take me there and get me a good deal. She was a hairdresser and gave up the business to go to university and study law. She gives me advice, telling me to keep my prices low to get the customers through the door. She tells me if they like me, they will come back. I reassure dad and agree to take the place.

I get home and phone the job centre for advice; they put me in touch with the WDA, who tell me about the Prince's

Trust. I have to be under thirty and on a low income to apply for a loan or grant of up to five thousand pounds. The interest rate will be 4 per cent, which is low, and I will be able to pay it back at an affordable rate. I ring up the WDA and am booked onto a course for the following week. I have to complete a business plan to apply to the Prince's Trust. I go to my parents the next day and tell them my plans. My dad offers to take me to the meetings; they run when the children are in school, so I do not need a babysitter.

My mother goes mad, telling me that I have enough to do with four children, and that I look tired all the time as it is. Dad tells her to let me have a go. "Look, if she tries and fails, then at least can say she tried. Otherwise, she will always wonder whether she could have succeeded." I am shocked at Dad's speech.

Mam replies that if I do it, I can manage the kids on my own because she is not helping. She adds that I have a part-time job, and that is enough.

I remind her that my boss has been dropping my days for the last month, and I cannot afford to lose thirty pounds a week. Mam asks how I am going to pick up the children from school. I tell her about the Prince's Trust and how, if I qualify, it means I will be able to buy a small car. I have to complete the forms straight away; the WDA have told me that the date of application will be logged. The funding will not be available until the following April, which is after my birthday, but they will honour it because I applied early.

Mam tells me if I don't slow down, I will break, and there will be no putting me back together. She adds that I already do too much, and she is worried about me. I tell her that I will be able to pick the children up from school and take them to the shop; there is a large staffroom. I can take the old television from my bedroom and their beanbags, and they can watch some videos until I finish work. Mam replies, "Do what you like. You always do, anyway." I am determined to prove to her I can do this.

Within a month, I have decorated the shop, and it is ready to open. Lorna and Mary offer to help paint in the evenings. Mam reluctantly offers to watch the children. I have to buy them an Indian takeaway meal for their efforts. Sophie has lent me five hundred pounds out of her savings, and I have promised to pay her back as soon as the Prince's Trust loan arrives. I have completed the business plan and have been awarded a loan of four thousand pounds. Repayments are 150 pounds a month. Sophie's loan has bought me second-hand washbasins and chairs, a till, some decorations for the interior, and the mirrors. The work stands were supplied by Lorna and Mary; the factory they work at had cut-offs of worktop and allowed them to shape them into shelves for me. I have painted and stencilled the shop, and I had the name of the salon painted on the windows.

My boss was not happy when I told her my plans. I offered to work two weeks' notice, and she told me to leave the same day. She owed me two weeks' pay and was reluctant to pay me back. I had budgeted that money to buy the showers for the basins. I rang ACAS, and she paid me but was furious.

I do not care; I did the right thing by her, and it was the least she could do.

I open for business within one month of signing the lease.

This was essential because I have to earn my rent, and I only have two weeks to do this. I have managed to get all my stock on a thirty-day payment agreement. For the first time in my life, I have qualified for a bank account, and I open a current and business account at Lloyds Bank. I ring the Inland Revenue, and a small business advisor is allocated to me for a year of free financial and tax advice. He arrives and informs me that I have to pay a class two tax for my stamp, pay tax for any employees, complete an end-of-year tax return every year, and pay tax on my stock. I wonder whether there will be any money left after all that!

Within two weeks, I have managed to make enough money to pay my first month's rent. Two weeks later, my loan comes through. and I repay Sophie and thank her. I also do all my family's hair for free because they have been such a big help to me over the years. With the remainder of the loan, I am able to purchase a small car; I passed my test over a year ago. I have taken on a member of staff, and the DHSS have a scheme going at the moment and will pay her wages and fund uniforms and travelling expenses. She is full-time and stays in the shop while I pick up the children from school in the afternoons.

Mam is still annoyed at me, but her workmates and friends are praising my efforts. I think that secretly, she is quite proud. There are a lot of people, including my ex-husband and his family, who are wishing me to fail. This only makes me more determined to succeed. My business advisor tells me that I will make a loss in the first year due to opening costs, and only 3 per cent of small businesses survive over ten years. Beating the odds becomes my new goal.

Running my own salon is hard work, as well as seeing to the children when I get home. I also have to wash and dry all the gowns and towels for the next day. It has been a year since I opened, and my stylist is still working for me but has just informed me that she is pregnant. Because of this, I have had to rearrange my holiday dates and have to go before she goes on maternity leave. I decide that I am going to surprise the kids. I have booked Benidorm; it is out of season, but I have been told it will still be warm. My family and friends are sworn to secrecy.

Mam has come around and is helping with the children. Andy and Sam have split up; she was sleeping with one of his friends while Andy was babysitting her nieces and nephews. Luckily she didn't get pregnant, but she constantly blamed him for it. I comment to Mam that she would be pregnant by her new bloke if it was his fault! Andy is gutted and is living back at home. The plus side of the split is he is allowed to wear his Wrangler jeans again. I joke that he is Andy Warm Balls once again!

Within six months, Andy has met someone new, and she is pregnant. Mam is thrilled and makes sure it is added to the grapevine that leads straight to Sam. Jonah is attending his first year at comprehensive school. He is turning into a stroppy teenager, and my mother keeps commenting that his hand is always down his pants. I joke that he is playing with his brains, and that I have to crack his bedsheets to get them off the bed. He is turning into a hypochondriac. First I have to take him to the doctors because he thinks he has a lump on his testicles; he has been having sex education lessons in school and is worried. I manage to squeeze him in on an appointment that has been booked for Eligh. We have to go in together, and I tell Jonah that in order to save him from embarrassment, I will tell the doctor about Eligh, get him sorted, and then give him privacy to see the doctor on his own. He agrees.

Their names are called, and we are told to enter room three. it's with Dr Jones, heo is very strict.

We enter the room, and the doctor tells us to sit down without looking up. He is looking at their records, and he looks over his glasses and taps the cards on the desk. He comments, "Right, then. I think we will deal with Jonah first."

Jonah looks at me for support, so I say, "Um, Doctor, Jonah is here because he thinks he has a lump on his left testicle."

The doctor orders him behind the curtain and asks him to remove his trousers. He explains that he is going to shine a torch onto his groin to take a look. I can hear Jonah squeak. "OK!"
from behind the curtain.

Eligh and I are trying not to laugh because we know the doctor will give us a row. Next I hear Jonah screech, "What are you doing?"

The doctor replies, "I am just moving your school tie out the way." he confirms that it is probably a cyst and is nothing to worry about. We laugh all the way home.

Next we have to go because Jonah keeps getting water infections. When we get to the doctor, he checks the urine, which is clear. This happens at least three times. On the fourth visit and urine test, the doctor asks Jonah to go into the waiting room because he needs to have a chat with me. Jonah looks terrified but agrees and leaves the room. I look at the doctor, puzzled. He says, "Tell him to stop playing with it." I am so embarrassed, but I thank him for the advice and leave the room. I collect Jonah and tell him we will chat in the car.

As soon as we sit down, he says, "Am I dying, Mam?"

I snap, "No. Stop playing with it."

His mood swings are getting worse. He flies off the handle with his siblings for no reason these days, and I have to shout at him all the time. He has become a stroppy teenager. I worry that I will not be able to cope on my own. I have started allowing Jonah and Eligh to stay up a little later than the younger ones because Jonah is getting bossy and loud, and he disturbs them. He thinks he is the man of the house lately.

A few weeks later, he is sat on the settee, watching television, when he shouts, "You sack of shit!" (I think.)

I am not having that! I run in the room and shout, "What did you say, Jonah?"

He crosses his arms over his head as if I am going to batter him and replies, "I meant bag! I meant bag!" I am speechless. I tell my parents the next day, and they are in fits of laughter!

Eventually, it is time for my well-deserved holiday. Dad has offered to take us to the airport to see us off. They will also keep an eye on the shop while I am away. I still haven't told the children. Everyone, including my staff, cannot believe that I have managed to keep it a secret for so long! In truth, I couldn't cope with them being overly excited. I send them to school, get them new clothes and trainers to wear, and lay them on the bed. I have arranged with the schools to pick them up at lunchtime. My parents, Lorna, and Sophie have come to the house because they want to see their reaction. As I walk the kids home from school, Jonah notices the cars outside the house. He asks me what is wrong and why everyone is at the house. I put my arms around him and say, "It's a surprise." We run the rest of the way.

When we get to the house, I turn to the kids and say, "Well, go on. Get showered and changed. We are going on holiday!" They are shocked, and I tell them that their new clothes and trainers are on their beds. Reality hits them, and they rush upstairs. I have never seen them move so fast! Four hours later, we are at the airport. I haven't taken them abroad on my own before, and I am anxious. We manage to find our queue, hand in our luggage, and go to departure.

While we are standing in the queue, Polly befriends a little girl about her age. I say hello to her and ask her if she is looking forward to going on holiday. Her grandmother is holding her hand. We arrive in departure, and Polly notices her new friend and asks if we can sit by her; I agree, and we sit down. The little girl's grandmother notices that I am on my own with the children. I can hear her whispering something to the girl's mother, but I take no notice because the boys are keeping me busy. As we get on the plane, Polly sees the little girl up ahead and waves to her. The grandmother looks at Polly and tells her to go away. She picks up her granddaughter and sits her in the window seat, and she gives me a stinking look before turning away. Polly and the girl start to cry.

I pick up Polly and hug her close. I comfort her and tell her not to worry because she will make loads of new friends around the pool. I am furious with the woman. I am guessing it is because she has noticed that I am a single parent. My children are well dressed, behaved, and polite. I settle the children into their seats, and we head off to Benidorm. Every half hour, Jonah's head pops forward (he is seated opposite us), and he says, "Cool surprise, Mam."

The holiday is great fun, despite the fact that Eligh and I have prickly heat and hay fever. We are on antihistamines all week. We attend a water park and spend all day going down the slide with the dingys on it. We all have on factor fifty sun cream. In the evening, my shoulders are glowing!

We visit an island, and I discover that Frankie does not like going on the boat at all. We spend most of the holiday at the beach. We are in the old town resort, and we walk around the harbour and look at the boats. Eligh is the daredevil of the bunch, and he loves the sea. Keeping my eye on all four of them is hard work. At one point, I have Eligh paddling far out in the sea; and he is only up to his knees, but I have visions of the water going deep suddenly. I have a tendency to think of the worst-case scenario. I think, *What happens if a shark is in there? I have to run in to save him.* I don't like the sea; the Jaws films have scarred me for life. Jonah is in there as well and keeps an eye on him.

The little ones are playing with a bucket and spade – well, they were five minutes ago. I turn around, and they are holding hands, running up the beach, and laughing. Every time I go to get them, they run farther away because they think it is a game. I decide to pretend to ignore them, thinking they will run back towards me. They keep running up the beach. I shout to Jonah and Eligh to stay there while I go get the others. I have to close the gap between Frankie, Polly, and myself, so I break into a run. They start screaming with laughter and keep running. I think, *I am going to kill these two.* I run so fast to catch them that my costume is stuck in the crack of my backside. I am dying with shame, and my face is beetroot! The beach is full, and as soon as I reach them, I quickly retrieve my costume to its correct position and tell them they cannot run away from me; we are abroad, and someone will pinch them. I walk them back towards the boys, sit them down on the beach, and will not let go of their hands for twenty minutes until they understand. Enough is enough for one day, and we head back to the hotel. We go shopping before heading home, and we get the presents for my family.

Within a month of returning from the holiday, my stylist goes on maternity leave. I have sorted out her pay with the help of my small business tax adviser. The college is asking for placements, so I decide to take on a learner; she helps on a Saturday, and her placements day is a Tuesday.

The new trainee is reliable and friendly. She is older and has a little girl around Polly's age. Within a month, I employ her part-time to cover maternity leave, and she has nearly qualified as a level three NVQ hairdresser. The business is doing well. I am working hard, and my parents are a great support. Mam comes to the house on Saturday mornings for me to go to work; this means the children can go out to play. When I get home, she has done my washing and ironing and has cleaned the house. She is a star. She refuses to put the ironing away, but I can live with that. The babysitter is due in two hours, and I am going out with the girls. I choose my outfit around my vast collection of shoes. Lorna has nicknamed me Emelda Marcos! I have earned a night out.

My friends have booked a minibus and are heading into town; it is one of the girl's birthdays. The bus is due back at twelve thirty, and I have arranged for the babysitter to get a lift home when he drops me off. The pub is really busy, and I start chatting to a guy by the bar; his name is Roger. He tells me that he has had his heart broken. He met a girl five years ago, and she had a son who was a few weeks old.

Roger took on the little boy as his own son and idolised him. Three months ago, she left him for someone else, and because he was not the child's biological father, he had no rights to see him. I sympathise with him, we talk all night, and I try to give him some advice. After many drinks, he ends up back at mine.

When I get in, Frankie and Polly are awake; they are getting older now and want to stay up to watch telly with the older boys. I go out to make myself and Roger a cup of tea.

When I come back in, Frankie and Polly are playing the "finger game" with Roger and giggling like fools. They are basically wrestling with their little fingers, and Roger is losing every time. They think this is great. Eventually, I manage to get them to bed, and we hit the sack as well. He is in bed before me, and the lights are out. I can feel that he has his jeans on and comment, "That's all right," although I am a little shocked that he doesn't expect sex. I say goodnight and turn over to sleep. A little while later, I awake to him snuggling up behind me, and I can feel furry legs. The jeans are off! In the morning, we snuggle under the covers and chat. After he leaves, I sit on the sofa and drink a cup of tea.

An hour later, Frankie and Polly get up and ask where the finger-game man has gone. I tell them that he had to go home. Frankie says, "Argh! I liked him."

As I finish my tea, I think, *I like him too.* He is the nicest man I have met to date, he loves kids, and we get on. He is ticking all the boxes. With a bit of work, he could be Mr Right!

I go into town every other Saturday and usually bump into Roger. We chat, and I have seen him a few times. I have also discovered that he is the broodiest man I have ever met. He is desperate for his own child. I explain that I have been sterilised and do not want any more children – four is enough. Although I know because of this it will never work out between us, it doesn't stop me from trying. I want a good father figure for my children first and foremost; it is the one thing money cannot buy. However, Roger is looking for a woman who will carry his child. and I am not it. Christmas is approaching, and I think this is another reason why I am trying to too hard to get his attention. The thought of spending another festive season single is too much to bear.

It is Boxing Day, and despite still being single, the children and I have had a great Christmas. Jonah is interested in film and video, and he asked for a camcorder for Christmas. I tried to get him a director's chair to go with it but could not find one. He is busy making films all day; his siblings are his actors.

I have arranged to go out with the girls tonight. Some of them are dating Roger's friends, so I have regular updates on him.

He has not impregnated anyone yet, and as far as I know, he is still single. I have a new outfit for tonight and am going to look extra nice, because I know he will be there. If nothing else, I am determined. I get to the club with the girls, and we sign in. It is freezing out, and my friend's mother keeps asking me if I want to borrow her cardigan. I feel like telling to fuck off because she has repeated it about thirty times, but I politely say no thanks again. As we head to the bar, I spot Roger. His friends have gone to talk to him, and he is looking over, embarrassed. We wave a hello and leave it at that. I like him but am not scraping his arse. My friend's boyfriend calls her over and is talking to her, so I am left to queue for the drinks. My mother has offered to have the children for the night because taxis are double the price, and so I am staying in my friend's spare room.

She comes back looking flustered as I hand her a vodka and Coke. She says that Roger is here with a date, and the boys have nicknamed her Slinky Tits. I tell her I am not bothered, and as I look over I see a girl staring over at me. I can't help wondering what he sees in her. She has black hair, tanned skin, and pale blue eyeshadow and eyeliner. Oh, yes, and lip gloss. I make an excuse and head to the loo; amazingly, the toilet is empty. I look at my reflection in the mirror and wonder what is wrong with me. I know I look good: I have lost weight, I am wearing a flattering pinstriped trouser and waistcoat suit, and it flatters my curves. My hair is curled and put up to perfection; I have strands strategically placed loosely around my face. I have clear (thanks to my nan's advice) porcelain skin and have put my make-up on to perfection. I am wearing my trademark matte red lipstick and brown eyeshadow, to compliment my blue eyes. I know that I look my ultimate best.

The toilet door opens, and in walks Slinky Tits.

I catch sight of her braless tits in her silky top. I think to myself, *Fuckin' hell. With those tits and that top, I don't stand a chance. She does not need to wear make-up, because no man is going to be looking at her face.* As I look up, she is looking at me. She has won and we both know it. I stand tall, holding my head up high as I go back to the bar. Time to get pissed!

I sit by my friends. I and only one of the other blokes from the group are single. Everyone else is paired off. He starts chatting away to me. He isn't bad looking, but he has tiny eyes and is a chocolate boy – not my type at all. He asks if I want a drink and is swooning in closer to me. I think, *Sorry, mate. I do not do friends and family.* I sit with the girls and avoid him the rest of the night. At about nine thirty, the bingo starts. I am on my seventh vodka and Coke and am miserable as I look over the room. Slinky Tits and Roger are playing bingo with his mother. It is half-time, and I cannot resist.

I go to the bar for another drink and purchase a gift for Roger. As I walk over, the lights come on, and they are chatting away. I approach him, and he looks horrified. I walk up and say, "Happy Christmas," as I drop the pink bingo blotter into his hand. I turn on my heels and walk off. The girls are in hysterics. Inside, I am hurt. I imagine Slinky Tits wearing a hairnet and rollers, and this cheers me up.

At the end of the night, I go back to my friend's place. It takes a while because it's sort of one step forwards and two back, while balancing the Chinese in one hand. There is more food over the pavement than in our mouths, and we laugh all the way. Eventually we get in and decide it's a pee and then bed for us all. She shows me to her spare room, says goodnight, and leaves. I switch on the light. "Fuck me!" I shout. "Have you got a ladder? The bed is huge!" I am not short but cannot sit on it. They are laughing and tell me to go to sleep. It looks like the bed on the storybook I used to read as a kid, *The Princess and the Pea*. I wonder if there is a pea under there. I take a running jump, hit my head on the headboard, lie down, and go to sleep. What a night.

The next day, I have such a hangover.

I get up early, and my friend drives me home. It's only a two-mile drive, and she texts her boyfriend the whole way. I am glad to get out of the car. I get in, shower, change, and head to Mam's to see the kids. They are up and watching a Disney movie. Mam asks if I had a good night. I lie that is was great, but she can see by my face that I am unhappy. She is the only one who can read me like a book. She makes me a cup of coffee and pats me on the shoulder. I thank her and lie that it is a hangover, nothing more. I do not want to talk about it. I sit on the settee with the kids and watch telly. I am contented; their love is unconditional, they don't judge me, and we are all happy.

We spend the rest of the day at my parents'. Eventually I briefly explain the previous night's events so Mam will stop giving me the puppy-eyed look. She tells me that I deserve to be treated better than that, and she reminds me how far I have come and how happy the children are. She adds that I don't need a man in my life. Frankie comes into the room and sits on my lap. I give him a hug, kiss him on the cheek, and look into his cute little face. I tell him how handsome he is, and he laughs. Life is good, and I am the luckiest person in the world. I have four healthy, happy children, and I wonder what am I moaning about.

A week later, Christmas is over, and the children are back in school, I have been in business for two years. Now that I have a credit rating, I decide to look into buying my council house. I am self-employed and discover that the only place that will consider me for a mortgage is the Halifax. They have a good interest rate at the moment. The mortgage adviser explains how it works. He tells me that all the mortgage company is concerned about is being able to recoup their investment if I cannot make the repayments and the property has to be repossessed. Because I am buying a council property and qualify for a twelve-year rental discount, I will be approved. He adds that there is an offer on at the moment, and the Halifax will cover the buying costs on the house. I get the house valued, and with my discount I can buy it for £20,600. The mortgage adviser tells me that I can borrow extra money for improvements, so I borrow £25,000. The repayments are £210 a month. It is cheaper than renting. I am now a home owner. I explain it all to Gemma when we next meet, and she looks into buying her home. The offer I had is gone, so she has to pay the costs, but she buys hers too.

I have £4,400 left for improvements, I have to spend it carefully and get as much done as possible. The first job is to take out the Parkray heating system. In the winter months, the house is always freezing, and it hasn't worked properly for years. I get a price to install gas central heating. It will be £2,300, and the plumber needs to change five radiators as well. We have agreed on a towel rail in the bathroom. He tells me he will agree to that price if someone will dig out the Parkray, because he doesn't want to do that job. I tell him the price includes the messy work, and I explain I have no one to do it. He reluctantly agrees to do the job. A week later, I have gas, the house is warm throughout, and it is much safer. The combi boiler is fitted, and I have hot water on tap!

Next, my dad and I visit a local DIY store and price the tiles. I am having a new bathroom fitted. The tiler is a friend's husband and offers to tile the walls and floor for two hundred pounds. I get the shell bathroom suite with a corner bath in champagne. The tiles are country cottage colour, with a plain but very effective boarder. The plumber has fitted a combi shower for me within the cost of the central heating. Two weeks later, I have a new bathroom, the blinds and accessories are terracotta, and it looks lovely.

I have enough money left to plaster the landing and stairs, including the ceiling, getting rid of the Artex fan design. Anything I can do myself is completed in the evenings when the children are in bed. I save hard and manage to get wooden flooring throughout the downstairs, as well as new carpet on the stairs and upstairs landing. Between work, looking after the children, and the DIY, I am shattered. I clean the house every Monday from top to bottom, and I am really proud. I turfed the back garden when I got divorced and added a fence around the side of the house, to keep the children safe. Except for the kitchen – I cannot afford to change this yet – the house and garden are looking great. I am pleased with myself and proud of my home.

It is summer. Jonah and Eligh are old enough to have a key and go into the house for an hour before I arrive home. This makes life easier all around. It is a hot, sticky summer's evening. I have finished work and can't wait to get in. Once I wash and dry the towels for the morning, I can have a nice bath and relax. It has been a long week. As I pull up to the house with the little ones, I see Jonah and one of Gemma's sons hanging out of Polly's bedroom window; it opens outwards. They are shouting and screaming, I see a water balloon hit the ground, and I am furious! As I approach the house, Eligh and Gemma's youngest nearly knock me to the ground as they run around the corner of the house. They are armed with water bomb ammunition. I take Frankie and Polly into the room, tell them to put the telly on, and shut the door. Then I scream at Jonah, Eligh, and their friends to get here right now and put down the water balloons.

I screech to Gemma's children, "Would you behave like this in your own home?" They shake their heads. I tell them to go home. Jonah tries to explain, but I scream, "Shut up! I have been breaking my back to get this house like it is." Gemma would not put up with it. There is water everywhere. I tell them that if the wooden floor is ruined, they will have to pay to replace it out of their Christmas money. They are gutted, and Eligh starts to moan that it was Jonah's idea. Jonah nudges him, telling him to shut up. I scream at them that they can start by getting the shop towels out of the car and use them to mop up the mess. I don't care if they don't love me, but they will respect me and this house. I also add that the telly is going out of the bedroom for one week.

They are gutted.

This is the worst punishment they could have. Eligh sulks in bed, and Jonah starts to howl like a strangled animal, saying, "But Mam! *South Park* is on tonight. The new song is on this episode – it's about salty plums!"

I think, *What?* as I carry the heavy portable out of the bedroom.

Jonah is hanging off my right leg, shouting, "No! Please, Mam!" I drag him along the landing as well, telling him to let go. He replies, "I'm sorry! Not the telly. Please!" I manage to get into my bedroom, which is next door. Exhausted I sit on the bed and tell him if he doesn't calm down, it will be two weeks. He is thirteen, for goodness' sake!

Two hours later, I am downstairs folding the towels in living room and watching *Coronation Street*. There is a tap on the door. I look down, and there is a coloured-in cutout heart. Jonah has written, "Sorry, Mam. I love you." I can hear he is still behind the door. I tell him to get to bed but add, "I love you too."

The next day, Frankie shows me his loose tooth before school; he has lost three in the last two weeks. I am a bit pissed at Mam because she increased the exchange rate for a pound a tooth. It was ten pence when I was a kid!

The house repairs and decoration have left me with no savings. The shop has hit its quiet spell; the takings are seasonal in my line of business. I hope Frankie's tooth lasts until tomorrow; I get paid my tax credits then, and I can pay out. Alas, Frankie loves money and is saving up. He proudly runs out of school smiling, minus the bottom tooth. I look down, and it is in his hand. I pick up Polly, and we head to the local shop. Money is tight, but I have managed to scrap together a pound and twenty-three pence in a moneybag; it is in one- and two-pence pieces. I enter the shop and work out that a loaf of bread and a pint of milk comes to a pound and nine pence exactly. I have enough left to get the little ones a five-pence Chupa lolly. My change will be four pence. I remove four pennies from the bag before giving it to the cashier. An Indian family owns the shop. I tell him he can check it, but it is correct. He stares at the bag of coppers and tells me that he cannot accept this. I remind him that its legal tender and it's the law – he has to! I pack up my goods and leave the shop. I do not care what they think. I have enough food to last us until the morning, and I cannot afford pride. Shit! I have forgotten the bloody tooth fairy!

The children have gone to bed, and Frankie has placed his tooth under the pillow. For the last hour and a half, I have scoured the house for a stray pound coin. Eventually I place the remaining four pennies under Frankie's pillow, including an IOU from the tooth fairy for ninety-six pence, explaining that she has been very busy tonight and ran out of money. She has taken the tooth and will exchange the note for a pound coin on the following night.

Frankie is the first to awake, and I hear an "Argh!" sound from his room, I get up and see him looking at the letter, the pennies in his hand.

I read it to him and explain that she is only little, so she cannot carry much money at any one time. I read the instructions on the note. He accepts this and is happy again. I tell Lorna, and she can't believe he fell for it. The following morning, Frankie is happy. He runs to his sock draw, pulls out his Spiderman wallet, opens it, and pops in the pound, telling me with a gummy smile that he has thirty-six pounds now. I laugh because he has more money than I do!

Jonah is a film fanatic and knows the names of the directors of all his favourite films. He knows exactly what he wants to do when he leaves school: be a film director. He has attended the local college's media department and become a regular visitor there. He also creates cartoon strips, has a vivid imagination, and is bright with a good sense of humour. Eligh is achieving great results in school, and he has a dry sense of humour. They bounce off each other and draw comic strip characters resembling themselves, emphasizing their worst features. Jonah always draws Eligh with a big nose; he has his dad's! Eligh draws Jonah with square knees; he follows the poison dwarf for those! Jonah also draws Polly with a big chin to wind her up, and Frankie is super hairy because he has loads of hair. Polly cries, "I do *not* have a large chin!"

The children still visit my former in-laws twice a week. Knobhead's mother hates me and the fact that I am doing well. They constantly interrogate the children, asking them for details about me and everything I do. She slags me off to anyone who will listen. The school term has just started, and I have to pick them up from the in-laws' house after work. I only speak to Knobhead's stepdad; he genuinely loves the kids, and we communicate for their sake. However, he is a coward and a childish man. He never goes out, and he times his wife when she goes to the shop or town. I can see how Knobhead has ended up the way he is, a prat and a bully.

I pull up outside to pick up the children. I have just changed my car for a Fiesta Sport, the new model. It is silver, and I love it. I know they are green with envy. I have it on monthly payments, and it will take four years to pay for it. As I pull up, I notice the glare of the binoculars in the window. I have been spotted. The children's grandfather comes up to the gate and asks me if he can have a quiet word. I tell the children to get into the car.

He then proceeds to inform me that when he was down at the shop earlier – I think, *What? You walked to the shop?* – a woman came up to him. He comments that he is not naming any names, but she commented on how scruffy the children were in school. I am furious and remind him that his stepson hasn't as much as bought his children a pair of socks since the divorce, and I have just kitted them all out in new uniform. I add they are always clean and tidy upon going to school, and I remind him that they are kids, so at the end of the school day, they may look scruffy. Frankie is so small that his uniform never fits him properly. I ask him to tell me who said it, but he refuses. I reply, "Well, if someone was talking about my grandchildren like that, I would have something to say about it." I ask him again who said it and tell him that when I find out, the person will have a piece of my mind. He is such a gutless bastard.

When I get in the car, Jonah tells me that the neighbour was asking him where he went for his birthday. When he told her he wanted money and we just went for a film and McDonald's, she laughed and said, "McDonald's? I go there all the time!" I am furious and tell him next time he sees that cheeky bitch, he has my permission to reply, "I can see that, lard-arse."

He replies, "No way! She is huge and might hit me!"

I tell him, "If she touches you, I will knock her out!" I am so angry. Jonah tells me to calm down. He makes me a cup of tea, and ten minutes later I tell him he is right; I can see that they are trying to wind me up. It's what they do: they want a reaction so that they can tell everyone, and probably even Social Services, what a psycho I am and that they were right all along. I decide to do what will hurt them the most: I rise above it and ignore them, because I am not that person.

Later that evening, I ring my mother and recall the evening's events, I tell her how angry I was and how I realised that it will kill them if I don't respond; they thrive on arguments. Mam agrees that I did the right thing and reassures me that no one thinks that about the kids. She reminds me that I have gained a lot of respect from my friends and neighbours over the years. I end the conversation, telling her I will see her in the morning. Tomorrow is Saturday, so she will be over as usual for me to go to work. As I leave that day, I notice scratches on my car, over the driver's door. I know it is them, but I think, *Fuck them. I am not reacting.* A month later, I get the door resprayed. It is simply not worth it.

Summer is nearly here, and that means holidays! I book us for a week away in Salou. My eldest two are now teenagers. Jonah has turned into Kevin, and Eligh is Perry! I need a break from work to recharge my batteries. I started dating a man from the neighbouring village about a month ago; his name is also Roger. I tell the girls, and we nickname my ex Roger One and my current guy Roger Two! My friends inform me that Roger One's relationship with Slinky Tits is over; she was two-timing him. They also inform me that he is expecting a baby. Apparently she was a one-night stand and has six children already. I tell the girls I am pleased for him, and I mean it. I know he will make a great dad.

Roger Two has just ended a six-year marriage and is gutted and on the rebound. I feel sorry for him and am like his counsellor. He isn't handsome, however he is a charmer. What impresses me most about him is the fact that he has two of his three children living with him. This means he is a good dad, and this is his best asset. I am feeling lonely and don't know if I can cope on my own any longer. I have loads of friends and a supportive family, and I love the kids, but I want someone for me. I daydream about cuddling up on the sofa watching a film, or going out for a meal with someone. Things that couples take for granted, I crave. I am going to make this work. I want to be in a relationship. I have been single for seven years.

Two weeks later, it is a Saturday night, and I am going out with Roger. My parents offer to give us a lift to the pub; we are only going out around town, but it is too far to walk. They haven't met him yet. This gives my mother the chance to interrogate him. She asks him what he does for a living, where he lives (she grew up in his village, so knows it well), who his parents are, how old his children are, and how his marriage broke up – all in the ten-minute trip. He answers all her questions in record time. I jokingly ask her if I can untie him and take the torch out of his eyes as we arrive at the pub. Dad laughs and Mam scowls at me, telling me not to be so cheeky.

My mother's advice to me the following day is that there are two sides to every story, and that he seems too good to be true. The children and I are at my parents' house for Sunday lunch; this is routine. Sophie arrives with her two as well. The house is noisy and crowded, and soon the conversation changes to something else.

Over the next month, I continue to date (counsel) Roger Two. He is an emotional wreck and is drinking too much. One night he calls me when he is drunk, telling me he has fallen down the stairs. I drive to his place and bring him back to mine. His children are older than mine and are able to look after themselves; it was OK to leave mine for an hour because Jonah is nearly fifteen, but I would not leave them all night. When I get him home Roger is drunk and sits on my settee. He tells me I should forget about him and that he will two-time me, because no one is ever going to hurt him again. I wonder if I will ever be good enough to fill his ex-wife's shoes. He moans that he has never been dumped before slipping into an unconscious sleep. I throw a blanket on him and go to bed.

This becomes a weekly event, and sometimes he sings himself to sleep. I decide I have had enough of his self-pity.

The morning after another episode of "poor me", I tell him enough is enough. I am not his mother and do not intend to keep running around after him. He is taking the piss! He apologises. I am going on holiday in two days with the children, and to be honest, I'm looking forward to a break from him. He offers to pick us up from the airport and suggests a fresh start when I return. He tells me that I have been his rock and that he would not have survived the last two months without me. I agree and tell him I will see him after my holiday. He jokes that I will come back white. I tell him to wait and see!

My parents drop me and children off at the airport. The kids are excited and cannot wait to go on the plane. We arrive in Salou around 10.00 a.m. the following morning. I had requested a ground-floor room with a sea view. We are taken to the fifth floor and have a view of the opposite hotel. I go onto the balcony and look down. We are so high up that I lock the patio door and tell the children they are not allowed out there. I usually get traveller's cheques, but this year my mother has managed to convince me to take cash because it is easier. I always take more than enough. We are half board, so we don't have to worry about running out of money for food.

We go to the welcome meeting to meet the holiday rep. Jonah and Eligh ask if they can play on the pool table in reception, and I agree. Frankie goes to watch, and this keeps them quiet as I decide what trips I am going to book for us. The holiday rep arrives and introduces himself. After a boring start, he tells us about the trips. I look at the Barcelona trip. It is all day and involves visiting an aquarium in the city centre. Polly is excited about that. He talks about the dancing fountains at the royal palace, which is included in the excursion. Polly and I decide to book the Barcelona trip, along with the water park and the Port Adventurer Theme Park trip.

I pay for the excursions and assess how much we have left. We are only there for a week, but Frankie's birthday is the day before we leave, so I will have to get him a present out here. After the meeting, I collect the boys at reception and purchase a safe key. We go back to the room to discuss what we have booked and what to do first. Everyone agrees on going to the beach. Before we leave, I take some money with me and put the rest of the spending money, along with the passports, insurance, and flight documents, into the safe and lock it, dropping the key in my bag. However, as I leave the room, I have this gut feeling that I should have split up the money and locked some away in one of the cases. I dismiss it, and we head for the beach.

After spending two cheap days, one at the beach and the other around the pool, I assess the cost as being around a hundred euros for both days. I check the spending money. I don't mind going home broke, but I want to make sure that it is going to last the week.

The amount does not seem right – I am at least a hundred euros down. I don't understand it, and I know the children haven't touched it. They have no need to, and I have the only key. I get that gut feeling again to split up the money, but I dismiss it and tell myself that I have counted it wrong. There seems to be no other explanation.

We go on the Barcelona trip, and it includes visiting the football arena, the aquarium, and the dancing fountains in the royal palace grounds. The children love the flame-throwing illusionists and the clowns around the palace, and the fountains are amazing. Polly's favourite place is the aquarium; we see hammerhead and blue sharks that are huge, and the aquarium is attached to the ocean.

The next day, we visit the water park and have a great day. We have one trip left, and my money is disappearing fast. I still cannot explain it because I am normally very careful. The Port Adventurer Theme Park is tomorrow, and I am nearly out of cash.

We walk to the theme park and have a great time, Jonah worries that we will not have enough money to get back, but I reassure him that I have some in the safe. Later, we get a taxi back, and I ask the driver to wait for me to get the money. When I get back to the hotel reception, I can hear a man screaming at the manager, "What is the fucking point of having a safe, when you bastards are stealing all my money out of it?" Suddenly I have an eureka moment, and everything falls into place. Someone has been robbing me! It is Frankie's birthday the day before we leave, and all I can afford to get him is a Spiderman lolly that whistles. Jonah says, "Mam, you can't just give him that." I explain that I am broke, and I tell them what has been happening with the money. I promise Frankie a proper gift when I get home. Frankie is sucking on his lolly and is happy.

Throughout the holiday, I have rung Roger Two. He doesn't answer the phone, or when he does, he says, "What do you want now?" I overhear him telling his friends that I stalk him. The cheeky bastard! I hang up on him. I am only ringing him to tell him that I have forgotten my phone charger, so before my mobile died on me, I wanted to give our flight details so that he won't be late picking me up. I think, *Fuck him. I have spare cash in the house for emergencies. I will get a taxi home and pay when I get there. That bastard can go fuck himself.* I have had enough.

Jonah approaches. He needs some more change for the pool table, and he asks if I am OK, I give him a kiss on the head and reply, "Yes, I'm fine." I tell him to hurry up and race him back to the others.

The evening before we leave, I use the sample pack of San Tropa tanning lotion. It has three steps: first a defoliater, next the moisturiser, and then the tanning lotion, to get a natural, all-over tan effect. It's a great job, if I do say so myself. The boys have gone down to watch telly in the lobby; Jonah is a great help with his brothers and looks out for them. Polly is lying on the bed, waiting for me.

The next day as we get on the plane, some of the passengers are giving me funny looks. They cannot believe how tanned I am. I have my holiday make-up on with coral lipstick, and my hair is scrunched and in a loose side plait. I have lost a little weight and am wearing a black halter-neck dress and slip-on, low-heeled shoes.

A few hours later, we land, pick up our luggage, and leave the airport. I am about to start looking for a taxi rank when I see Roger Two stood there. He has a black eye and is feeling sorry for himself. He said he had been waiting for hours and left me loads of messages. He looks me up and down and asks if the tan is real. I reply of course. The boys are not sure because they weren't there when I applied it, and Polly doesn't understand the question.

He asks why I didn't answer any of his messages. I reply that I forgot to pack my charger. He struggles to get into the car and tells me he was jumped on a night out, and that it was all Stuart's fault. Stuart is his mate, a womaniser and sex addict. He explains that Stuart was chatting up a girl when her boyfriend arrived with a load of mates. He tells me that Stuart ran off, leaving him to take a beating. He is waiting for me to sympathise and ask him if he is OK, but I do not. We get home and unpack the car, and the children go up to bed. Roger asks if he can stay over; it is late, and he tells me that the journey has worn him out. I agree he can stay, and he tells me to forget sex tonight because he is not up to it with his injuries – and he knows what I'm like! I ignore the remark, lock up the house, and tell him I am going to bed. I feel pathetic and lonely, because of this I cannot seem to go through with dumping him.

Roger has started to come to the house in the evenings after work three nights a week. I cook a Sunday lunch on Monday because I work a Saturday and go out therefore, and I'm too hung-over to cook the following day. My mother would never forgive me if I made her redundant and did not eat her famous Sunday lunch; she enjoys feeding the family. I always make a special effort with my cooking, and I have heard that the way to a man's heart is through his stomach. I sit Roger opposite me at the head of the table, and the children sit in the middle. Roger always comments on how Frankie uses his knife and folk; he is left handed like me and does not have strong hand control. He is small for his age, and looks much younger. To be honest, I have never noticed this before.

Frankie doesn't like Roger. I put it down to jealousy and the fact that he and the older boys do not want a father figure and are happy with the way things are. Roger asks if there is more gravy, and as I leave the room to get it I hear Frankie shout, "Mam! He is staring at me!" I enter the room, and Frankie adds, "Why do you always sit me opposite ugly?" Everyone except Roger laughs.

When we go out drinking together, Roger looks around the pub and eyes other women. When I confront him, he insists that he is just "people watching". He then says he was thinking that if I lost weight, I would be the smartest girl in the pub. He tells me that I have a pretty face. Then he reminds me that his two ex-wives were size eights and that he is struggling to enjoy a sexual relationship with me. He says to be honest: he likes his women slim, and I am not. I am a size fourteen. I think to myself, *OK, I can diet and lose weight – and then dump you, you cheeky bastard!*

Roger and I go to the Social Club on a Saturday night with his friends, as couples. Roger still insists on his boys' night out every Friday, so I continue to see my friends every Sunday. We always have a laugh, and we have been going to the nearby village each week for a few years. There are several busy pubs that are no more than ten metres apart; this is important when you wear heels. They are always packed, and we know most of the locals. The nightlife consists of different types of people. The local men consist of twenty-five- to thirty-year-olds who are in various relationships and seem to swap partners every other week. Then you have the thirty- to fifty-year-olds; these consist of mostly divorced individuals who are in different stages of the mid-life crisis. They are mostly balding and squashed into a size thirty-four waist pair of Levi's and a checked shirt, which is tucked in to disguise their man boobs and pot bellies. They are confident individuals. Their normal chat-up line is something like, "If you play your cards right, I might shag you!" I call these men the non-committers.

The women are mostly middle-aged and newly divorced. They have been on the divorce diet and sunbeds, to disguise the stretch marks, and they are confident that they look amazing. They also believe that they can still pull off the leather miniskirt and matching boob tube. These women are fresh meat for the non-committers. The other type include the women who have been divorced for several years and wised up. We have learnt to befriend the non-committers, realising that they make much better friends than lovers.

My friends are all dating non-committers. Their boyfriends live off them all week, but they are not allowed to look or touch their phones. They follow them around like puppies to ensure no other women can get near them. There is no use trying to talk to them because they will never end the relationship, despite what advice I give. I tell Sophie about my friends and their partners. She asks if it sounds like me and Roger. I reply, "No, of course not!"

Time has passed quickly. I have been dating Roger for almost a year. Polly likes him coming around, and she wants a father figure in her life. Her own father hardly sees her or the boys, but they do still visit their grandparents on a weekly basis. Jonah and I joke about his nan's daily routine. She is a bitter, nasty individual, and the only time she leaves the house is when she is going to the shop to restock on flagons of Strongbow for her and her husband. Jonah and I joke that when she goes to the shop, it is like a day trip for her, and going to town must feel like a holiday.

A week later, Jonah comes home and tells me he could have died earlier. He went to his nan's after school, and she croaked, "All right, Jon?"

He replied, "Hi, Nan." He went on to tell me that she had her coat on, so he asked her, "Off out, are you?"

She replied, "I'm going on holiday, Jon. I'm off to town."

He looked over at Polly because she had arrived before him, and she said, "It was funny! I didn't know it was a secret!"

I reminded him that she is only a child and that her nan should grow up. They constantly ask the children whether Roger stays the night. The children quickly learn to say as little as possible and always tell them no. They are sick of being interrogated by them.

It is nearly Christmas, and the shop is really busy. I am working full-time, attending all of the children's Christmas plays, shopping for presents, decorating the house, and trying to maintain a social life. I am exhausted. I am also constantly worried that Roger will two-time me. I am stressed out, and it affects my health. I suffer with a bad stomach and get terrible cramps.

It is the Saturday before Christmas. The shop is packed. I get up in the morning, and suffering severe constipation. the cramps ane so painful. My mother comes over to have the children in the morning, and she observes how pale I am. I am always pale, but today I am like a ghost. I tell her what is wrong, adding I have to go to work because I cannot let down my customers.

I work all day but need to run back and forth to the toilet; the cramps are excruciating. The customers are concerned but say, "Once you have done my hair, you should go home. You look awful." I feel like I am dying. My senior stylist and friend, Ali, tells me when I get home, I should sit over a bowl of boiling water and let the steam "get in there". I reply if I do that and Jonah sees me, it will go viral on YouTube the same night. She laughs.

Eventually, after taking every constipation tablet I can find, I head home. Ali asks me to let her know I'm OK later, and I tell her I will. When I get in, I head straight to the medicine cupboard and take some of Eligh's Senicot and Laxtilose. I return to the living room and sit on the sofa. My mother asks if I am OK, and I tell her, "No – I'm in agony." I ask if she will watch the kids if I have a nap. I feel like I am sat on an egg. Twenty minutes later, I come around, and Mam tells me to go upstairs and try to go to the toilet again. I sit onto the loo. and in between the cramps and cold sweats. I pray to god, the angels. and anyone up there to take away this pain. I am rocking back and forth. Around ten minutes later, I have an urge to push down. My back passage feels like it is going to split apart before I eventually pass the blockage, and it hits the lavatory like a torpedo.

I am exhausted, relieved, and thanking God at the same time. I am also bleeding, but I'm so relieved. I promise myself I will not take my health for granted again, and I decide to sort out my love life. I go downstairs and tell my mother the good news. Then I text Ali, "The rocket has been launched!" My mother tells me how relieved she is;

she was about to call an ambulance. I tell her that I am fine now and thank her for watching the kids. I also reply that the babysitter will be here soon. She cannot believe that I am still going out. I joke, "My motto is that I work and play hard." I also know that Roger has got tickets to the band in the club, and if I don't go, he will be flirting with anything in a skirt. As he says, he isn't getting hurt again, and I am not ready to let go. I shower and change in record time, Roger picks me up, and we head to the club.

Ali rings me. She has just got my message and thinks I am hilarious. She also cannot believe I am out already. I explain that Roger has to be the first in the place. I sit in the Social Club with him and three old men. I tell her I will see her tomorrow for our girls' night out. Roger asks me what I want to drink, and I ask for wine and lemonade. I tell him that I have been really ill today and so cannot manage cider tonight. He returns from the bar with a half a Strongbow. He says if it's good enough for his mate's girlfriends, it's good enough for me. The truth is he is too fucking tight to pay for wine.

An hour later, all the couples have arrived and notice that I am quiet and not drinking much. I tell them that I have been ill and not been able to eat all day. I manage a few sips of my cider and cannot drink any more. Roger is happy it's a cheap night for him; he doesn't even ask me if I am OK. Around nine thirty, I start to get some more stomach cramps and head for the loo. Two elderly ladies are leaving the toilet as I approach, crouched over in pain. They ask me if I am OK, and I tell them that I am. Before I enter the toilet, I overhear them whispering, "Perhaps she's having a miscarriage."

I enter the toilet. The only available cubicle is the one without a window. I manage to undo my trousers and sit on the seat just before I empty the entire contents of my stomach, including every laxative I have taken that day. The smell is like a three-week-old corpse has left my body, and I am nearly sick. As I sit on the toilet I can hear that the loos have filled up, and there is a queue outside. They are wondering what is taking me so long. I have to flush the loo three times, but the smell is still pungent. As I open the door and leave, I hear, "Argh! Who died?"

Thanks to Roger, who refuses to leave early, I have to sit there all night, enduring comments and stares whilst he watches the band. I cannot eat or drink anything, and I just want to leave.

The next day, Roger and I get up early. He leaves because he has to go to the Club for his ritual Sunday morning drink and do the tote. I wonder how he can go straight back on it after the night before.

I am feeling much better, and later in the day, I go up to Mam's with the children for lunch. In the evening, I am going out for a catch-up with the girls. I manage to eat dinner, and my mother comments on my weight loss. Over the last six months I have lost three and a half stone. I vowed the day Roger commented on my weight that I would diet, and then he could fuck off, but I have to admit despite the way he treats me, I still like doing the couple thing and am reluctant to give it up.

As I am getting ready to go out in the evening, Jonah enters the bedroom. He comments, "Mam, how thin are you?" He has only just noticed that I have lost weight. I laugh at him. He tells me I look like a skeleton. I look in the mirror, and I am thinner than I have been since before having him. My collar bone is protruding, and I look bony around my neck and shoulders. For the first time, I can fit into size eight jeans. Roger thinks I look great – but it has not stopped him from eyeing up anything in a skirt!

I go out and meet up with Ali. She gets the first round in. I drink wine and lemonade when I am out with the girls because I am paying for it myself, and I have what I like to drink. Roger turns up with Stuart and a few of his mates. This is not his usual haunt, and he looks drunk and upset. The pub is packed, but he won't tell me what the matter is, so I ask Stuart. He tells me not to worry about Roger; he isn't worth it. Stuart and I have become good friends. He is married and has never flirted with me. I am out of bounds due to him and Roger being mates, anyway.

I show Stuart the girl who has been staring at me for weeks now. I ask him if he know her, and he looks at her and tells me he doesn't, but I shouldn't worry about it. I am guessing that she is newly divorced. She is tanned, nearly black with white hair, isn't skinny, and covers up her full figure with a long, ankle-length coat.

Roger overhears our conversation, and his colour drains from his face as the woman walks up to him and says hello in a posh voice. I ask him how he knows her. He shrugs his shoulders and tells me he's going home. He leaves the pub. I am puzzled and decide that I can't be bothered to follow him. Ali asks me what the problem is, and I tell her about the woman. She says that she knows her; she will do a bit of investigating and let me know. She reminds me tonight is our night, so I forget about it. We move onto the next pub.

The following week, I am at work, and Ali comes in on her day off. I assume that she has come to pick up her scissors because she often leaves them behind. She asks if she can have a word. I apologise to my client and follow her into the staffroom. She says, "That bastard has been seeing that girl behind your back!" I ask her what is she on about. Roger is at my house every night of the week now, except for Fridays when he goes out with the boys. Ali tells me that she has a friend who confesses that she has been seeing him on Friday nights for the last few weeks, and that he had taken her for a meal last Thursday. I think back to that night and remember that he told me he was working. Ali says that Roger rang the girl, and he told her that he panicked on Sunday, thinking that she was going to tell me. That's why he was upset and went home.

I ring Roger and confront him. He denies everything. I tell him to fuck off because it is over, and I slam down the phone. An hour later, he pulls up outside the shop. He asks me to go with him for five minutes and have a chat. I agree only because I do not want my customers listening to my private life. I get into the car and tell him to pull up to the side of the road. Roger has a smug grin on his face and he asks me when I go shopping, will I get him some new pants. I reply, "What's the fucking point? You don't keep them on long enough." He thinks this is hilarious. I scream at him. "I will *never* be treated like that ever again by you or anyone else!" I am furious. He admits that he did see her, but she was hanging around him, and he was drunk. I tell him to fuck off because it's over. Then I get out and slam the door. I am gutted.

Ali warns me that the other woman's best friend is the hardest woman in her village and will smack my face in if she sees me when I am out. I remind her that I haven't done anything. Ali suggests going out in her village this weekend; she knows what pub she will be in and advises me to have it out over there, or else I will have to face her in our usual haunts, in front of all our friends. I agree. I have no choice.

The following week, Ali and I enter the woman's local pub. It is half empty, and we get a drink and take a seat. A minute later, the woman walks over and asks if she can talk to me. I take a deep breath and tell her she can. She explains in her very posh voice how Roger wouldn't leave her alone and kept pestering her for a date. I ask her if she has slept with him. I still can't believe he would do that to me. She smugly replies that she has, adding that she went to his house on Friday nights and met his children. Little details slot into place, like how he stopped ringing me on Fridays and would not answer the phone if I rang him. Also, he would ask me if I was going out every week to make sure he didn't get caught.

I tell her, "The worst thing is that I was there for him when he got divorced, and this is how he thanks me." She replies that she can see how upset I am, so she will step aside for me. I am furious. I reply, "You are welcome to him." The cheeky bitch!

Just then her phone rings, and Roger's name is on it. She looks at me, and I tell her to answer it. She answers, purring, "Hello, Rog. Guess whom I'm talking to?" I hear him ask who, and she says my name.

I take the phone out of her hand and say hello. He asks if I am OK. I tell him, "Yes, we have just been discussing how small your dick is, and we have nicknamed you Mini Me!" Before he has a chance to comment, I hang up the phone. I hand it back to her and walk back to Ali. She asks if I'm OK, and I reply, "I want to go home."

In the taxi, Ali's tries to make me feel better. She says that I am the opposite of that tart; she is all fake, fake tan, fake eyelashes. She's a mess. I am humiliated, and I also realise that it means I am going to be alone again. Ali tells me that I should look in the mirror. I am a pretty woman who has a lot going for her. She adds, "You are even prettier than me." This is a massive compliment because Ali thinks she is gorgeous!

Three weeks have passed since I have split up from Roger. I have arranged to go out with the girls on Saturday; Dad has offered to be my taxi. The evening passes slowly, and I drink too much. As the night ends, I am glad to get into Dad's car. On the way home, I ask, "What is wrong with me?"

He tells not to be silly. All his mates at the pub think I am lovely, and everyone likes me. He says that I was too good for Roger. Mam's opinion is that she could see he was a waster, and I am better off on my own. She adds that she will never forgive him for hurting me like that. The children are blissfully unaware that I am thoroughly miserable. Polly asks why Roger doesn't come to visit anymore, and I tell her that we have split up. Frankie and the boys are pleased, they tell me, "He was a moany git, anyway."

Roger tries to contact me at least twice a day on the phone and at work. I ignore him. He has tried to talk to me when I am out. Stuart confides to me that Roger and the woman are not getting along; she spotted a love bite on his neck that she didn't create. I laugh and tell him it wasn't me.

Despite feeling like crap, I make the most of my new figure. I have always been told I have a good pair of legs, and I wear a denim miniskirt and some fake tan to enhance them. My dad tells me that I inherit them from my mother, and that was what attracted him to her. He adds that thin ankles is a must for a cracking pair of pins. He is dropping me off at the pub and picking me up tonight. The girls are all coupled up, and I am going out with a friend and client from the shop who lives in town. I go out and meet her, and I am drunk by the third pub.

Roger One is out and asking to talk to me. Eventually he pulls me outside and tells me he has missed me. I haven't seen him for over a year. I ask him about his new baby, and he tells me he has a son. I congratulate him, and he adds that he has heard I am single now, and so is he. He goes on to say that he and the boy's mother have split up. Although he adores the baby, he hates her. He also adds that because she already has her hands full with six children, she allows him to see his son as much as he likes. I tell him that I have to leave because my friend is in the pub on her own. He requests my phone number and asks if he can take me out on a date, and I agree. After all, I have nothing else to do!

Roger One and I agree to meet up the following week. I meet him at his place because I don't want to see anyone that I know. We go for a meal and chat, and it is nice. He tells me that he has bought a house and has completed all the DIY work himself, which has been keeping him busy. He asks me what happened with Roger Two. I fill him in, telling him that basically, he did the same to me as he did two-time me. I laugh about it.

He is serious when he looks at me and says, "It's not funny, though, is it?"

I reply, "No, it isn't. But humour is how I cope. I was taught to laugh at myself before anyone else can."

He apologises to me for treating me so badly. He tells me I am looking great, and he asks me if, after the meal, I would like to see his new house. I reply, "Why not?"

Roger One shows me around his home. He says that he has decorated it throughout. I tell him that it is lovely. He pulls me close, kisses me, and tells me that we could get back together. My children would be welcome here, and we could stay every weekend. He adds now that he has his son, we could be a family. He asks me how the children are, and this makes me smile. I tell him that Frankie still mentions the finger game. He laughs and says that his mates told him that I was getting married, so he didn't try to get in touch with me.

I tell him I have to be going, I gave him a kiss on the cheek and ask him to give me time to think. I have just come out of a relationship and don't want to get hurt again.

Ten minutes later, I am sitting in my car and thinking to myself, *Eighteen months ago, I would have been over the moon with this news.* I ask myself if I can take being hurt again, and if I want to go from the frying pan and into the fire. I think about the kiss and whether I can rekindle the feelings I used to have for him. I ask myself what those feelings were and realise they were pity. I don't think I cared for him at all; I simply wanted to help him. The reason I wanted him so badly was because I knew he would be a great dad to the kids, but was this enough? What about me? What do I want? I realise it is not Roger One.

A minute later, my phone starts to vibrate. Roger Two is calling me, and I answer the phone. We arrange to meet. Later in the evening, when I get home, I text Roger One and tell him I'm sorry, but I've had a think about it and realise that I cannot go back to him.

I meet Roger Two, and we talk. He tells me how much he has missed me, and he didn't realise what he had until it was gone. The story of my fucking life! He says that his dad thinks I am one in a million and that he was a fool to risk throwing away a hard-working girl. He says he wants a fresh start.

I reply, "If I go back to you, it has to be different." He asks how I have been getting on. I tell him I have been decorating and saving for a new kitchen; it is the last big job to do in my house. He offers to fit one for me if I buy it. I say that if he does, I will have enough left over for fencing all around the house. He offers to do that for me as well. I think about how much it will piss off the posh bitch if we get back together. I also think about how much money I will save by having Roger Two back.

This outweighs the humiliation of telling family and friends that I have taken him back. I also have to admit to myself how pathetic I have become. I cannot face being alone anymore. I was on my own for seven years, and I have had enough. I tell the children about my decision. Polly is happy, but the boys are not. My mother is worried, so I tell her when he finishes doing up the house, I will finish with him to keep the peace.

Roger Two does as promised and finishes the jobs in the house. I have a new kitchen and fenced garden within two months. He tries to charm Mam, but she isn't having any of it and keeps asking me when I am going to dump him.

I have sex on tap again, and I enjoy snuggling up on the settee with a glass of wine and having an adult to talk to in the evenings when the children are in bed. He has given up his boys' nights out. Roger has suggested moving in together, and he tells me that his daughter has just moved out because they haven't been getting along. There will be room for all of us, and the living costs would be much cheaper. We discuss selling my house and paying off his mortgage. We would be much better off with two incomes. I want us to be a happy family. I want to be the same as everyone else.

A month later, we are living together. My mother is hurt and upset. I have promised the children a puppy if we move. I have not changed their schools because Jonah is in his final year, and the younger children's friends are there. I work near the school and can pick them up and drop them off before and after work. Dad sees that I am happy and forgives Roger Two; he tells Mam that I have been on my own long enough, but he warns me to be careful when I pay off his mortgage when my house sells. I tell him I have thought it through and will make sure my name is on the deeds and that a written agreement is signed and witnessed by a solicitor. Roger is money mad, and I don't trust him in financial matters. I have worked hard over the years to benefit my children, not him or any man.

Polly makes friends easily in our new village. She is the youngest and loves having a father figure around. Roger is good with her. Frankie is jealous and tells me he doesn't like him. The older boys joke that Roger is so lazy that he drives to the sofa and jumps on. We laugh about this on our trips to school and work. Roger goes to work early and is always in his spot on the sofa when we get home. To them, it seems as if he doesn't move off it.

The boys are teenagers and are too old to start taking rules and orders from Roger. He wants them to keep the house spotless all the time and not eat any of his snacks, but this is not going to happen. The arguments begin!

Every Saturday I take the children to my parents. They live around the corner from our old house. They go out with their friends while I am in work, and they have said that they don't want to be left at the house to listen to Roger moaning. After work I pick up the children and have a cup of tea and a chat with Mam. This annoys Roger because he is a stickler for time and hates me being late. He expects me home and ready to go out by six thirty on a Saturday. It is ritual that we go to the club, and he has to be one of the first ones in there. I do not rush home, and this causes arguments every week.

I go to my parents' as usual the following Saturday, to pick up the children. Mam meets me in the hallway, and she looks concerned. She tells me that Jonah is sleeping on the settee, and she thinks he is drunk! I ask, "What makes you think that?" She tells me that he came in and said he was tired and was going for a lie down, but he had better lie on his side in case he is sick. I look into the room. Jonah is snoring on the settee.

Mam ushers me into the dining room and puts the kettle on. Dad is sat at the table, listening to his music; he loves jazz, Michael Buble, Queen, and any country music. We have been brought up with this playing in the background. Mam loves her soaps on the telly and hates music. Dad tells me his version of what Jonah was like when he came through the door. I tell Dad that he shouldn't laugh and that I am going to give Jonah a row when he wakes up. Lorna walks in, and Mam tells her about Jonah. She thinks it's funny and reminds me of what we used to get up to at his age. I tell her to be quiet and not repeat everything I did to the kids all the time. She has already told them about my market days and the toilet experience, and I could kill her for that. However, she has always kept my darkest secret.

An hour or so later, Jonah stirs, and I decide it is time to have the chat. I ask him if he has been drinking, and he denies it. I tell him that we can all see that he has, and we can smell it on him. Lorna, Mam, and Dad are in the room. I am bad cop, and they are standing behind trying not to laugh.

I ask him where he got the drink from. Eventually he gives in and explains that he and all his mates supplied a bottle each. He got his from his nan's, a flagon of Strongbow. His one friend had a bottle of Lambrini, another one had four cans of lager, and the last friend had a bottle of vodka. They went up the mountain for the day to drink it.

I comment, "Oh, great. And you have mixed your drinks!"

He replies, "No, no! I drunk them all separately!" I am speechless. Lorna, Mam, and Dad are hysterical. Jonah goes to the bathroom to be sick. I tell them to stop laughing because I have to punish him. Lorna reminds me that he is in the bathroom spewing; that, along with the hangover he is going to have, is punishment enough. I eventually agree. We decide to leave him at my parents' to sleep it off. I don't want Roger to find out, giving him something else to moan about.

We have been living with Roger for seven months now, and the children are still asking me about the puppy they were promised. Every time I bring the subject up with Roger, he tells me that we have a dog. He has a four-year-old mongrel called Patch. I remind him that I promised them a puppy. I have brought the children up to understand that if I promise them something and can afford it, they will have it. I have never gone back on my word, and I don't intend to start now. I have a plan!

On the school run, the children and I discuss what puppy they would like. I remind them (especially Polly) not to mention it to Roger. Eligh tells me he wants a Bassett Hound, and the others are not bothered. We cannot find a Bassett Hound breeder in the local area, so we choose another breed. Eligh is adamant that he is naming the dog, and it will be his. He has wanted a dog of his own for years. I drop off the children at school and head to work. It has been quiet in work all week, so I have spent spare time looking in the free ads for puppies. The other condition from Eligh is that it is a boy.

Lorna comes into the shop for a chat, and I tell her my plan.

Lorna loves animals and offers to help. I call the breeder and ask if she has any boys left. She has one and describes the pup, and I tell her I will have him. We arrange to meet her the next day at a petrol station, which is halfway, to collect him. Lorna and her friend offer to pick up the puppy for me and take it to her house.

The following morning, I give her the money for the pup and tell her I will ring Roger and explain that Lorna has a friend who is getting rid of a pedigree puppy because she and her partner have split up, and she has to move back home. I will say that her younger brother is allergic to dogs, so she has to find him a home, and she wants fifty pounds for the puppy. We agree not to tell the children about the plan.

Lorna thinks I am mad and questions what we are going to do with the puppy if he says no. I tell her to stop worrying. The only other people who know about the plan are my parents, Sophie, and Andy.

I ring Roger and explain the plight of this poor girl and the opportunity of a bargain. He is a miser and cannot resist. He replies that if Lorna brings the puppy down tonight, he will have a look at him. Lorna has already left to pick him up. On the way home, I pick up two bottles of wine for Roger; he is more agreeable when he is drunk.

Three hours later, Roger has drunk a bottle of wine and is happy. Lorna arrives with the puppy. Roger is smitten and tells Lorna that he thought it would be a scrawny little thing, but at fifty quid it is a bargain. Lorna is laughing and says she agrees, though she knows he cost me £450. I call the children downstairs before he changes his mind. We have a new puppy, and Eligh names him Fred.

Although I live with Roger and pay money into a joint account for the bills, he doesn't know what I earn. My business is just that – mine. He has no say in the running of it and does not get to look at the books. This is handy because I have discovered that Roger is a skinflint, a miser, and one of the tightest men I have ever met. If I have a good week in work, I have to stash money away for a rainy day, in case the children need anything. I am determined that they are not going to suffer financially because of my decision to live with Roger.

Although Roger likes to think he is the boss of the relationship, he is not. I have learned to be one step ahead of him on most of his decisions, and I pre-think about how to get the result I want. An example of this would be the decorating ideas. Roger blames his ex-wife's taste for the colour scheme in his house. However, he's proud of the living room because he chose the colours. It is the most normal colour scheme in the whole house. I have changed the dining room from tangerine orange to cream and white, and I added a few plants. The boys' bedroom was mint green, but it is now pale blue and white. The bathroom has gone from a disgusting raspberry pink to white with peach accessories.

We are about to decorate the living room, and he insists on choosing the wall colour. I give in and tell him he can choose it if he wants. He heads to his all-time favourite shop, B&Q, with a huge grin on his face like a ten-year-old. We arrive at the store and look at the paints. He chooses carky beiges and mustardy creams, and they are disgusting. I tell him that a cottage cream or winter white is much nicer for the living room, but he insists he is choosing. Forty minutes later, he chooses the cottage cream, and we leave the shop. He is happy, and so am I.

When we meet up with friends that night (yes, at the club), he is tells all his mates that he had his way, and the colour looks lovely on the walls. Yes, he knows best. The Social Club is the only pub in the village; it is near a cluster of small shops, which consists of a post office, newsagents, and a Spar. There is another shop that is now empty; Roger tells me that it used to be a DIY store but closed a few years ago. Nobody has been able to change or buy the lease off the local council since then. I tell him it would make a great hairdresser shop. We discuss me opening another shop. I also ask our friends what they think when we go out to the club. They have lived here all their lives and tell me that they have never had a hairdresser here. It would be a goldmine and so handy for all the locals.

The next few weeks are spent ringing the local council offices, arranging to buy the lease, and designing my new shop. Roger has agreed to help, and Lorna, who has just been made redundant again, has asked if she can manage it. Her friend Mary is getting her down and always follows her to every new job she gets; this will break that cycle. I agree because I need someone whom I can trust. She is not and never will be a hairdresser, but she has agreed to attend college and complete a beauty NVQ course and a nail art evening class. This means she can earn her wage, and the shop can offer both services. Lorna tells me what wage she wants. It has to match her last job, or it will not be worth her working. It is more than I can afford because I have to employ a hairdresser as well, but she is my sister, and I need someone I can trust. I agree.

Two months later, with Roger's help, we gut the premises and have a new hairdressing shop. He tells me that this one is both of ours due to the fact that he has helped to create it. What he means is the profits are to be shared. He hasn't actually put his hand in his pocket and paid for any of the refurbishment. I have looked into and enrolled Lorna on her beauty courses at the local college. She will attend them in the evenings, and I have pay for them I have managed to employ a hairstylist who will work alongside Lorna, who will manage the shop. I will work one day a week in the new shop.

Two weeks later, we open the new premises. I soon discover that although everyone thought it was a brilliant idea, they do not support the new shop. In the first two months, I cut the prices to get customers through the door. The new business is being supported by the old one. I am wearing myself out by trying to take as much money as I can to cover everyone's wages.

Every time I see my mother, she tells me how tired I look. She is the only one who notices. She also reminds me that once I break, there will be no putting me back together. She pleads with me to slow down. I know she is worried, but I cannot – I have too much riding on this. I reassure her that I am all right.

She also tells me that Roger expects too much of me and is always on the phone, screaming at me all the time about me being late.

Mam says that I am racing around to keep him happy, and she is worried that I will have an accident. She tells me that he doesn't treat the boys right, and Frankie, who is the most placid little boy, hates him. I know she is right, but the house has just sold, and I am financially and emotionally tied to him. I push Mam's worries to the back of my mind. I think back to the time he cheated on me and how upset I was. The person who was there for me was Mam, and she saw how hurt I was. I know she has never forgiven him for that. I know he will never hurt me like that again. People only have the ability to break your heart once. I have healed and am stronger now. I will never trust him 100 per cent.

I am also aware that I always have the boys' backs and guard them from Roger's mood swings. Polly is a girl, and this seems to make all the difference because she gets away with murder. Roger's excuse for this is that she talks to him, and the boys do not. I wonder why? All he does is shout at them! I have discovered he is like this with his own children as well: his two girls adore him, but he has little time for his son. His eldest daughter has announced that she is pregnant. Roger is over the moon and comments, "Make sure it's a girl, I prefer girls." Surprise, surprise!

My days off are Sundays and Mondays. Roger has become more controlling since I moved in with him. The sale of the house has gone through, and I have paid off his mortgage and added my name to the deeds. We are in the process of creating an agreement and new wills, to ensure I do not lose my money if we ever split up or if one of us dies suddenly. Roger has taken out two life insurances on me, insisting that if I have an accident, he will give one of the payouts to my children. I do not believe him, so unknown to him, I have a separate one for the children. Only my parents know about this, and they are happy that I have financially secured the children's future. So am I.

Roger tries and fails to fill up my Mondays. I have always taken my mother and Sophie out for lunch that day. Lorna is usually working or out with her partner, and because we have never been allowed in her house, we do not feel that we can call in on her at any given time. I clean the house and complete all the household chores on Sunday, after our weekly visit to B&Q and the local garden centres. My lie-ins are non-existent because Roger cannot lie in bed. His motto is, "One up, all up."

Mam has been telling me lately that she cannot keep her food down. She has confessed whilst out for lunch that it has been going on for several months now, and she is too scared to go to the doctor. I have asked her how she has managed, and she tells me that she can suck whole-nut chocolate and has been living off that. I remind her of when Sophie had her gall bladder removed, and how the symptoms seem similar. I also mention the fact that she eats loads of butter on her toast, and the fat is the worst thing for it. I tell her to go to the doctor and get it sorted out, or else the acid will erode her teeth – and she doesn't want to be gummy at her age. We laugh, but Mam looks worried. I make her promise to go to the doctor, and she finally agrees.

I drop her off at home, and Dad is there listening to music, Mam puts the kettle on. I ask him if he knew about her being sick, and he replies that he has been telling her to go to the doctor for months; he even made appointments for her, but she gets mad and will not go. I ring the doctor, make an appointment for the next day, and tell her to make sure she goes. I remind her that she has promised me. I sit in the car and am ashamed that I have been so busy with everything that I did not notice.

I ring Mam the next day after her appointment, and she tells me that she has to go for tests. When Sophie hears about it, she insists on going to the hospital with her; she only works part-time and can rearrange her shifts. Sophie is the eldest and likes to take charge of any situation. This pisses off me and Dad because it comes across as being nosy rather than concerned. Mam tells us it's OK; it's Sophie's way of dealing with things. We shut up for her sake.

A month later, Mam is diagnosed with cancer, and we are all devastated. From the day she found out she had what she has always called the C-word, she looks terrified. I can only describe every photo of her taken after that day (Dad snaps her on every occasion) as her looking like a rabbit caught in headlights. A week later, I visit her, and we are being really positive. I tell her she is the fittest, strongest person I know. As we talk, I notice a strong, pungent smell and ask her what it could be. She replies, "It's me. You can smell cancer, you know." Her hand goes up to her mouth, and she is embarrassed. I tell her it isn't that bad; I was just wondering what it was. I feel terrible and try to reassure her, but after that, she always talks to me with her hand over her mouth. I feel like crying, but I don't. I have to stay strong for her and help her get well. She will overcome this – she has to. How will I ever manage without her? She is so much more than just my mother. She is my friend and my rock.

A few months later, life goes on. Between work and running around to keep Roger happy, I go to visit Mam in hospital; she has had a stent put in. When I arrive, Dad tells me that it has ruptured. She has to be fed with a tube into her stomach. This breaks my heart because I know that she loves her food. The next day they move her to a larger hospital in the city. I haven't been there before, and Roger has to take me. Work has been busy, and I stop off to pick up some things for Mam, which means I get home forty minutes late. This is late for Roger – I get timed. He is furious. I explain that I had to pick up some new nightgowns for my mother, and I wanted to get her some magazines. He is putting the greasy spaghetti bolognese dinner he made me into the bin and screaming that I just don't give a fuck. I apologise for being late and tell him I am not hungry anyway. I am secretly relieved that I have not had to eat his "speciality". He tells me to fuck off and adds he is not taking me to see my mother. I tell him that I don't know the way to that hospital, and I beg him to take me; she is ill, and I really want to see her. He refuses. I tell him I will go myself, but I am reluctant to leave the boys, who have all gone upstairs. They have had McDonald's on the way home because they also dislike Roger's cooking.

I get in the car, and realise I don't have a clue how to get there, and I start to cry. Eventually, I ring my mother and tell her I am so sorry, but I can't make it tonight. She tells me that she understands that I am busy and not to worry. I promise her I will be there tomorrow.

I go back into the house and head straight to bed. I will never forgive Roger for this, and I cry myself to sleep. The next morning, he makes me coffee, but I tell him to fuck off. He grabs hold of me and tells me he is sorry; he took it too far last night. I start to cry, telling him I am really worried about her and wanted to see her last night. He apologises and promises to take me to see her tonight. I wash, get ready for work, and call the children, and we leave. Life goes on as normally as possible. I don't want to upset the children.

Later that evening, we pull up at the hospital, and I cannot stop crying. He apologises again. I get out of the car and enter the hospital. It is an enormous building, and it takes me twenty minutes to find her. I go into the room and kiss her on the cheek.

She wakes up and looks so ill. The first thing she says is, "Are you OK, love? You look so tired." I burst out crying. She holds my hand, and I apologise to her for not being able to get here last night. I tell her I just couldn't make it. Roger is quiet.

I tell her how worried I have been about her and ask if she is OK. Roger makes his excuses and goes for coffee. I let her talk, and she tells me how scared she was. She says that she has been hallucinating, and she could see gypsy faces all around the bed, men and women. I tell her not to worry because it's the medication she is on. I hold her hand and tell her I love her. She tells me she loves me too. I realise how we never say this to each other, but now I need her to hear it more than ever. I am scared. What if she doesn't make it? Visiting time is over too soon, and we have to leave. I kiss her again and tell her I will see her soon. She is already asleep.

As we get back to the car, Roger grabs my hand and apologises again. I pull away, telling him to forget it. He says that he didn't realise that she was so ill and that I would be so upset. I remind him that she is my mother, and I think she is going to die. He squeezes my hand again. We drive home in silence, and I vow that even if I decide to forgive him, I will never forget this.

A month later, Mam slips into a coma. When the doctors ruptured the stent in her throat, it hit the tumour and – in a way, fortunately for her – it spread upwards to her brain. If it had spread downwards, the doctor said that it would have gone into all her organs; this apparently is a more prolonged, painful death. The doctor is explaining that they are going to give her nil by mouth, and this includes water. We are allowed to sponge her mouth to give relief, but that is all. He tells us she will not be able to hear us talking to her. I look over his shoulder at her face. She is trying her hardest to say something; her lips are moving but she cannot manage to get any sound out. I know she can hear everything he is saying.

We all take it in turns to visit and chat to her. I promise her I will always look after Dad. I tell her not to worry about him because he will be OK. I know this will be her main concern, and I feel the relief wash over her face and see her physically relax. I know she heard me. I tell Sophie, Andy, Lorna, and Dad. Andy's grieving comes out in the form of denial and anger. He cannot believe that they cannot do an operation or something to cure her. I ask the children if they want to see her and say goodbye. The boys do, but Polly is scared when she goes in; she panics and starts to cry. Roger picks her up and hugs her, and I am grateful that he is there. The boys chat to her and say goodbye. I wonder if they understand how final this is. Two weeks later, she passes away. My mother has died.

At her funeral, Dad and I stay strong. Andy is still in shock and angry that she is gone. I let the older boys attend but decide that Frankie and Polly are too young, and so I send them to school. Dad and I compare the time we haven't seen her to feeling like when she used to go on holidays with her sister; it feels like she is going to walk through the door any minute. Mam asked to be cremated, and Dad has honoured all her wishes, making sure that we are all happy with the arrangements. Sophie chooses a song by R. Kelly called "If I Could Turn Back the Hands of Time". My auntie remembers the songs Mam always said were her favourites, so we also choose those. Dad cannot part with her favourite jumper or coat; it is like she is still alive.

I keep my promise to my mother. I now clean Dad's house and do his washing and ironing, as well as running two salons and caring for four children (well, five including Roger). Dad has turned into a mixture of his old self and Mam since her death. Before she died, we never really chatted to him. Now we feel that we have to go in and have a chat because he is lonely. Jonah and Eligh stay at Dad's quite a bit; it keeps him company, and they cannot stand living with Roger.

Jonah and Dad have become close, and he reveals that Jonah's started asking him for advice on some health concerns of his. I ask him what Jonah worried about. Dad tells me it's nothing for me to worry about. He gives me an example of Jonah's last concern, telling me he rang him the other day and told him that he was worried because he was really constipated. He told him that after a while of sitting on the loo in pain, his eyes bulged a bit, and then he managed to open his bowels. Although this was a great relief, he was still worried because Elvis died on the toilet. Dad says he reassured him that – although he didn't know that – in the end, Elvis had to take drugs to get up in the mornings because he was addicted to prescription painkillers. He said that Jonah was happy with this explanation. Dad swears me to secrecy, telling me that Jonah won't feel like he can tell Dad anything if Dad betrays his trust. I agree after laughing my head off.

Frankie also stays at Dad's on weekends. I visit morning and night before and after work, and I take supplies for the boys. Lorna has said she will hoover and polish at Dads if I do everything else. Her reasoning for this is that the boys are there, and she is not cleaning up after them. I cannot argue with that. If there is one donkey in a family, I am it!

Jonah has started university, and Roger is thrilled. As soon as Jonah leaves, Roger makes plans for a bigger bathroom, knocking through into Jonah's room. He tells me Jonah has moved out now. I try to explain that he will be home at term time, but Roger won't have it, saying that he has had enough of Jonah keeping him up all night. Roger is a light sleeper, and Jonah doesn't give a shit. Roger goes on to say that he will have an accident on the way to work if he doesn't get proper sleep soon, and he has had enough. Jonah is distraught and confides in Dad. Dad tells him he will always have a roof over his head as long as Dad is alive.

I am between the devil and the deep blue sea. I can see that Roger has a point when he says that Jonah keeps him awake. Over the years, I have learnt to sleep through Jonah's racket. I tell Roger that Jonah is my son, and this is his home. Roger will not change his mind, and in order to enforce his decision, he starts to work on the bathroom straight away. I reassure Jonah that I will always be there for him, and Dad and I will always have his back. I sort out his lodgings, and we settle him in. He settles into uni life quickly, meeting new friends and having the time of his life.

Jonah and Dad become closer than ever over the next year, and Jonah stays at his granddad's every term time. Secretly, I am glad he is away from Roger and the moods. If Jonah needs money or food, Dad or I make sure one of us can take it to him. I tell my father not to tell Roger anything because it keeps the peace, and he agrees. I feel like I am living a double life.

The second shop has been open for a year and a half, and it is still not making a sustainable profit. Lorna has qualified in the beauty courses. I have kitted out the shop with a beauty couch, a wax pot, and a nail bar, but she doesn't seem to have enough confidence. The only day we make money is on the day I am working. I work hard all day, and at the end of the week, the stylist and Lorna are holding their hands out, demanding to be paid and knowing that they have sat on their arses all week. I have also been told that the stylist has been doing mobile as well, the cheeky bitch. I am furious – talk about taking the piss!

A week later, Lorna asks if I can attend a meeting after work. I wonder what is happening. When I get there, they make me a cup of tea and are joking around. Eventually I ask them what the problem is, and Lorna pipes up, "Oh, nothing. We just thought because we have been open a while now, we were due a pay raise."

I reply, "No way!" and remind them both that they do not even cover their own wages, let alone the running costs of the business.

When I get home, I tell Roger about the meeting and the mobile rumours. I also tell him that I am worried about my hands. My knuckles are enlarged, and I think that it may be the onset of arthritis. I have looked into doing my PGCE teaching qualification. This is a precaution, as a back-up career. He tells me that I am doing too much now, and it is a good idea to do the PGCE, but I must give the second shop up first because it is a chain around my neck.

I have to agree with him. The following week is spent enrolling on the PGCE course and obtaining shadow teaching hours at a local college. I then inform Lorna and my stylist that I am selling the shop. I tell the stylist that she has first refusal, and I am asking five thousand pounds for it. She tells me she wants it, and within a week, she has paid me and the shop is hers. Lorna is furious, but I am sick of carrying her.

Three months later, I am attending the same university as Jonah. I go one day a week for two years. On my uni day, I have an insight into Jonah's lifestyle. He is enjoying life and is happy. He has made lots of good friends and is pursuing his passion, documentary film making. He updates me on his ideas and what his next project is going to be. I take his shopping to him before my course starts. I know if I give him money, he will spend it on his busy social life. A month later, Jonah announces that he has a girlfriend and wants me to meet her. Her name is Carla.

Since my mother's death, Sophie and I have become closer. Lorna is still bitter at me for finishing at the salon, but she has a new job in a local healthcare trust and is now a carer. Lorna doesn't have children and has always joked that she prefers animals to kids any day of the week. Sophie and I still go out on Mondays, despite Roger's efforts to fill up my time.

Eligh is about to finish school and start college. He has become distant and withdrawn. I know that he does not like staying in the house, and I cannot blame him, Roger has got rid of Jonah and has moved on to moaning about Eligh all the time. The poor kid cannot do anything right. Three weeks later, I come home to Roger screaming, "He has done it again!" I ask him what the matter is, and he screams, "He has moved the shower head."

I think, *Big fucking deal.* I remind Roger that it is a movable shower head. He screams that if he keeps moving it, it is going to break, and he is practically spitting in my face. I tell him to get a fucking grip. This is the last straw for Eligh, who can hear the row from his bedroom upstairs. He is packing his stuff. Roger has stormed into the room like a girl as Eligh and Frankie come downstairs. Eligh comments that he cannot live with the prick any longer, and he asks me take him to Granddad's. I make Frankie and Polly come with us and drop Eligh at my father's, explaining about the row and how Roger needs to get a grip. Amazingly, Dad sticks up for Roger and says it is hard taking on someone else's kids, especially when you know they don't like you. I remind him that it is Roger's fault.

Polly asks to go home because she is tired. Dad agrees that Eligh can stay with him for a while. Eligh is unpacking in the bedroom. as I go up the stairs to speak to him and get Frankie, I overhear Eligh telling Frankie, "Mam chose Roger over us years ago." I enter the bedroom and tell them both that it isn't true, and I will always be there for them. I also tell them that they do not understand and that I am torn because Polly loves Roger.

I kiss Eligh and tell him I love him. He replies, "Yeah, right." Although things settle down, Eligh refuses to come home. His granddad says he can stay with him as long as he likes, but he has to keep the bedroom clean. Eligh is a slob. I clean the house to save arguments and make sure Eligh has everything he needs. He has become quite crafty and will ask Dad for money, and then ask me. Later in the day, when I see my father, I have to pay him back. This goes on for several weeks and is getting expensive. Between buying food for Eligh and Jonah, they are bankrupting me. I tell Dad to stop giving them money; if he does, I am not going to pay him back. I also tell the boys to cut it out. It has taken all my savings to keep them, and I am struggling. I joke to the girls at work that if Roger knew how much they were costing me, we would be divorced.

As the months slip by, Frankie spends more and more time at my father's. He tells me, "Our house doesn't feel like home anymore." His granddad's house is his home now. I feel sad I am losing them. Roger is happier these days; he has succeeded in pushing my boys through the door. Although I have always told him if he makes me choose between him or them, it will be them, it doesn't feel like it. Polly loves Roger, and if we go shopping or go on holidays, he spoils her and lets her take her best friend with us so she has company. The boys stopped coming on holiday years ago. I put it down to them being teenagers and not liking the sun, but in truth I cannot blame them. For them, spending a week with Roger would be like torture.

Even when we go away with Polly and her best friend, Roger is great for the first three days. But as soon as he realises that we are spending money, he sulks, argues with me, and storms off for no reason. I call him a twat! But Polly won't have a word said about him.

Roger has been moaning that I have gained weight again, and he tells me if I wanted to go to the gym, I could "make time". I tell Sophie about it, and she says, "He is a cheeky bastard and should look in the mirror." Roger is not a fitness fanatic or muscle bound. He is a classic middle-aged, bald, pot-bellied man with man boobs. He thinks because his arms and legs are skinny in comparison (this is not a good look), he can eat what he wants. Sophie reminds me that I am only a size twelve.

Roger has also been commenting on my saggy boobs and stomach, and he constantly makes comments like, "Watch that you don't trip over your nipples when you get out of the shower." Polly thinks this is hysterical. He tells me that we are comfortable, so why don't I treat myself and look at getting a boob job or my stomach done? I am amazed and look at the cost online. I tell him how much it will be for a tummy tuck and boob job. He replies, "So long as you get a loan. We have no mortgage now. Go for it!"

An hour later, Harley Street calls me on the phone and tells me I could go in for a free consultation next week. I tell Roger, and he nods his approval. Three months later, I am led to a hospital in London I have a tummy tuck and a boob job. My saggy 36B cups are transformed into 36DD. My stomach has been taped tight together with a sticky bandage, and I have to wear a support belt for six weeks, I cannot shower for two weeks and have to use wet wipes. Jonah sees me at my father's after the operation and comments on my thin stomach (it is still taped). It has totally transformed my shape.

Three months later, Roger has bought me a second-hand running machine, and I exercise every morning. I make the time.

I have to admit that the surgery has given me confidence. I feel like I have the figure I had before Jonah, but with larger boobs that are firm and attract a lot of attention. I have lost weight, and Roger has proposed to me. We are engaged.

Polly has a boyfriend, and he visits most nights. He is a nice lad, but I am concerned that he is two years older than her. They have been dating for nearly a year now, and Polly still hasn't forgiven me for making her go on the pill. I have told her she is not living my life. I want more for all of them, but especially her. Men can walk away, but women cannot, and she is my girl.

Seven months later, Roger and I tie the knot. It is a quiet affair, and we invite our children and their partners, a few family friends, and our siblings and their significant others. Roger has a granddaughter, and he is over the moon because it's a girl. He has told his daughter and her partner that he will babysit any day except Saturday – he will not miss going to the Club. I have been trying to get him to venture somewhere different, but his excuse is always, "Let's just go with the flow," or, "When we get to the Club, we'll see what the others want to do." They never want to go anywhere different.

Six months later, his other daughter announces that she has a boyfriend and is bringing him to the house for us to meet him. She has been dating him on and off for a few years, and he works in the same factory. Her sister has informed us that he was married with a young son, but he has finally left his wife for Sally. It is a hot, sunny day, and we are in the garden talking to the neighbours while we wait for them to arrive. We hear a loud, screeching noise and car engine, so we go to investigate.

An electric blue Subaru with blacked-out windows has pulled up outside the house. Out jumps Sally and her fella. He is a forty-year-old man who, apart from a bit of fluff in the middle, has a strawberry-blond spike all around his head to disguise his baldness. He looks like an old version of Bard Simpson. Sally shouts, "Hi, you two! This is Ken."

I cannot look at Roger. We say hi and invite them in. Sally and Ken become regular visitors. They are allowed because she is his daughter. Occasionally they stay a little too long, and Roger gives massive hints for them to leave. I tell him how rude he is, but he doesn't care. Ken is in his mid-life crisis, and I cannot work out whether Sally actually loves Ken, or whether she simply wanted him because he was married.

A few weeks later, on their next visit, they pull up on a brand-new motorbike with matching outfits that are black with red stripes, as well as matching boots and helmets. It must have cost them a fortune. Sally looks terrible, but Ken is on another level. His pot belly is protruding in his suit, and the helmet has flattened his spikes, showing several moles in the fluffy area. I offer them a cup of tea as an excuse to leave the room.

Polly comes into the kitchen and spots me giggling to myself. She says, "Oh, you've seen Mork and Mindy, then, have you?" We are in stitches. Three months later, Sally announces she is pregnant. The bike and Babygros have to go!

Roger's daughter's are like chalk and cheese. Sally is the loud, abrupt one. All through her pregnancy, she tells anyone who will listen that if her sister can go through labour, so can she, and she isn't worried at all. Several months later, she gives birth to a daughter. When we reach the hospital, her mother and Ken look exhausted and tell us that she screamed the hospital down – and they have told her not to come back! We meet Roger's second granddaughter, who is the double of Ken and has a mop of red hair.

Roger's friends have discovered caravanning and have joined the club. Some of his friends have tents, so this means that we have a break from the Social Club. Although it is fun, I find it hard to get there because I work Saturdays. Because of this, if we go, Roger and Polly go earlier, and I meet them later. He has invested in a cheap caravan. This is the only time Eligh will go back to the house; he minds the dogs. I order takeaway for Frankie and Eligh before I leave for the campsite.

Roger has been on the phone at least twenty times, wondering where I am. I get there around seven thirty, they are all drunk, and Roger is furious. I sarkily apologise for not bringing the helicopter, and everyone laughs except him. The only time we have sex these days is make-up sex, and the next day, he has to tell everyone we did it. He is like a fucking child. The caravan comes out every weekend, whether I want to go or not, and he reminds me that we have to go with the flow.

I have completed my PGCE. There hasn't been a spare minute in the day for me for almost two years. My graduation is coming up, and I think of my mother and how I wish she could be there. Lorna and Roger come to my graduation. Lorna snaps a few photos; it's a nice day, and we sit out in the sun. She has forgiven me for losing her job and is enjoying her new one. I think she has found her calling. I joke that I never thought I would see the day that she would be wiping arses! She replies, "It's not that bad, and I always wear double gloves!"

Eligh has started college and is doing a fine arts diploma. He is very talented but does not know what he wants to do.

I tell him that he would be good at architecture and remind him that he has achieved all his sciences, maths, and English GCSEs. He tells me that he doesn't want to do that. Frankie is also good at art and is in his last year in school. He still has one-to-one teaching because he is dyslexic. The teachers tell me that he is working to the best of his ability. Polly is going through her stroppy teenager age, and she is hard work. She has a new friend whose parents have just split up, and Polly tells me that she shouts at her mother and is really cheeky to her. I tell her if she spoke to me like that, I would go mad. Polly knows her boundaries and is careful not to break them.

I apply for a teaching job and am successful. It is one day a week, and I teach fourteen- to sixteen-year-olds on a learning pathway hairdressing course. I love working with this age group. Stroppy teenagers are my speciality! I work for an independent company, and my manager is down to earth and very supportive. She helps me with anything I need to know, and in return I offer to cover parent evenings and advertising events if I am available. Roger tells me that my pay can go into the savings account and will help to pay for the monthly instalments on the new caravan he intends to buy. He always has a way of channelling my income into his pocket. Although we have a joint account, if I spend any money, within the hour I get a phone call to ask what I have spent and why. He is tight as fuck!

Six months later, life is plodding along. I am as busy as ever and try to fit in seeing Sophie and Lorna on my day off. They have noticed how little time I have to spend with them and comment on how many times Roger rings, wanting to know where I am and how long I am going to be. Dad has had the date for his new hip operation. It is in three weeks, and he adds that it would be nice to talk to me because I never have time to sit down anymore. I apologize and say I will tomorrow, before rushing out of the door.

The weeks pass quickly. Dad's operation goes well, and he tells me that for the first time in forty-three years, his legs are the same length. The surgeons have new machinery now, and this time they were able to successfully get the old, false hip out and replace it. He is booked in to have his knee done next, and then he can go back to work and book another diving holiday. This is his passion; he loves deep-sea diving and is planning on returning to Egypt and diving in the Red Sea. He reminisces about his last holiday there, telling me that the hotels are enormous and the food always gives him the squirts. I thank him for that bit of information, and we both laugh.

When he asks me if I want to watch the videos he has at home (he has several), I decline. They are home videos of him underwater in a wetsuit, doing the "OK" sign all the way through it. Dad gives a running commentary as we watch (suffer) it. At one point, he approaches a turtle and comments, "That's a turtle." When there's a fish, he says, "That's a fish. Look!" It's more boring than going to the Club or caravanning. I like my new friends, but they do not want to go anywhere fun or exciting!

Dad is recovering well from his operation, but he has had to go for tests because he keeps getting water infections.

A month later, he tells us that he has cancer cells in the bladder, but we shouldn't worry because he is confident that the doctors have caught it early, and he will be OK. A month later, Dad has a biopsy on his bladder. He tells me how embarrassed he was when a young, spotty-faced nurse had to slide a tube up his willy. Although it didn't hurt going in, it made his toes curl when they pulled it out. I am imagining my father's screams and think back to the time when |Mam used to cut his toenails. He used to howl before she had chance to get near him!

Unlike my mother, Dad is not scared; he is positive they will cure him. His job has kept him going since her death. I am so grateful to his employer for keeping him on. I remember the time he suffered from depression. He has always promised himself that he would never sink so low again. I am glad that he has the strength to cope without her by his side. I tell him I love him and am proud of him. Sometimes you just have to say it out loud.

Jonah is still dating Carla. She is a lovely girl but has mood swings and a temper. Jonah is in denial about my father's cancer. He tells me he knows his granddad will be OK. My father has been like a dad to the boys, and Jonah tells me he would be devastated if anything happened to him. I reassure him he will be OK, and we go for coffee. Jonah confides in me about Carla, and I give him the best advice I can.

Four months pass quickly. I am busy with work and coping with both households, as well as running around after the children and Roger. Dad's illness is subconsciously pushed to the back of my mind. The shop is busy, and I am enjoying work. My teaching job involves travelling to different salons throughout the day. I love the independence driving gives me. I have just changed my car and enjoy singing to my favourite CDs; this washes away all the stress in my chaotic life. It also stops me from worrying about Dad and how quickly his illness is taking hold of his body. The cancer has spread to his liver and kidneys, and although we are all really worried, Dad is staying strong. He gets admitted to hospital on a weekly basis now.

I make sure all his washing and ironing is done, clean the house, and change his bed. This causes arguments between Roger and me; he shouts that Sophie and Lorna should be helping out and reminds me that I also have a brother. He also feels the need to remind me that I work six days a week and have more children (he calls them sprogs), whereas Sophie and Lorna only work part-time. He adds that I am his wife, and I should be there for him (I do all the housework and his washing and ironing). He reminds me that I am not cleaning behind the pictures, and it is causing spiders to come into the house – work that one out!

I reply, "If he wants the back of the pictures cleaned, he can do it his fucking self!" I remind him that I made a promise to my mother that I would look after Dad, and I am doing it whether he likes it or not. I am sent to Coventry yet again!

It is two months later, and my father is losing his battle with cancer. He doesn't want to know how ill he is and is in denial. Therefore due to patient confidentiality, the

Occupational Health Board cannot give us any information on how long he has left. We know that he is terminally ill. He keeps his sense of humour to the bitter end and manages to have us in stitches with every hospital visit.

He is in agony most days now and finally accepts that he is dying. He tells Sophie that he does not want to die in hospital, like my mother did. He wants to go home. Sophie arranges a meeting with the occupational health nurse and he tells her his wishes.

The nurses and other staff make the necessary arrangements to get a hospital bed into his house, and they set up the twenty-four-hour nursing care. I will always remember his face when he came home. We put him onto the bed, and I look at him. He is smiling. I ask him if he wants me to take off his coat and shoes. With his arms crossed, he replies, "Nope, I'm home." He tells us all that he loves us. We are advised to let him talk because it is taking all his energy to say what he wants. My aunt and uncle (his brother and sister-in-law) are also heartbroken. We sit and talk about the old days and all the funny times we had, and we remember my mother.

The boys stay with him until the end, but Polly is too upset and is afraid to see him. Roger suggests we take her home and reminds me that we have to finish decorating the bedroom because we have been up here all day! We go to the house, and Roger moans until I help him complete the painting.

In the early hours of the morning, I get a phone call. Dad has died. Sophie asks if I want to go see him before they take him away. I reply that I can't face it. I add that I saw Mam, and that is how I remember seeing her. She says that it is OK. I ask her to look after the boys, and ask if they are OK. She tells me they are OK, and she will watch over them. The truth is I know Roger will moan if I go up to my family. My father has just died, and he wants me to finish decorating the fucking bedroom in the morning. I cry myself back to sleep.

I arrive at Dad's the following afternoon; I leave Roger with Polly in the house. Sophie, Lorna, and Andy are there. Andy is crying, and Lorna is comforting him. Sophie asks me where have I been, and I tell her that Roger wanted me to finish the bedroom. Lorna and Sophie exchange glances. Andy asks, "What is his fucking problem?" I tell them I know he is a twat. I ask where the boys are, and Sophie tells me that her husband has taken them to KFC for food. I give her the money to cover their meals and put on the kettle.

Sophie is talking about the death certificate and the will. We sit around the table and agree from now on, this is about us and only us. No spouses will be involved in our decisions. We also agree that everything will be split four ways evenly, because we know that this is what our parents would have wanted.

Sophie then asks if she can give me some advice. I ask her what is it, and she says, "Look, Lauren. I know that Roger doesn't hit you around like Knobhead did, but the mental abuse is the same." She adds that he doesn't give me a moment's peace and hates me bothering with my own children.

Lorna says, "Dad has died, and Roger has you decorating the fucking bedroom. Who does that?"

I agree and tell them, "Now that Dad is gone, the children only have me. Things are going to change."

In the next month, we discover that Dad had more money than we realised. His motto was, "Don't keep all your eggs in one basket," and he lived by that rule. He had about seven separate accounts and ISAs, amounting to a nice little nest egg. Roger keeps asking if I know anything about the amount I will receive. I keep telling him no. He has plans to buy a little flat with it and rent it out. I have my own plans!

Roger has bought a new puppy. It was the breed he wanted, and he thought that because we were coming into a few quid, he would treat himself. The dog is gorgeous, and although Roger thinks it is his dog, Benji immediately prefers me. I shower him with affection, and in return Benji gives me the loyalty and love that is missing in my marriage. He becomes my only reason to go home. Polly stays at her boyfriend Jack's house most evenings, and the boys live at my father's.

Lorna, Andy, Sophie, and I have agreed that Dad's house has to go up for sale. I have a quarter share in the place. Roger suggests offering my siblings a pathetic amount for the house. I tell him, "No, we are not doing that!" He is not happy, but he can piss off. He is expecting me to rip off my own family! I have been renting my business premises for eleven years, and though the owners have promised me first refusal, they are not interested in selling the place. I want to do something with my inheritance that will make my parents proud of me. I am also worried and need to make sure that the boys always have a roof over their heads.

The next day, I see a business premises with a flat above for sale. I rush to the estate agent, get the details, and arrange a visit the following day. It needs a bit of work, but this is the answer to my prayers. I put an offer in, and the estate agent rings me the next day to tell me that there are several buyers interested in the building, but if I write a letter to the owners, they will consider me because they would prefer a local business owner to purchase the property. I go straight to the library, type out the letter, and give it to her an hour later. She laughs when I tell her, "I hope I get it. I want it more than anything." I go on to tell her all the plans I have for the place. She tells me that she has never met anyone as determined as I am, and she will put in a good word to the owners. I thank her and leave.

A week later, the estate agent rings me and says, "Congratulations, it's yours. The owners have accepted your offer!" I am overjoyed. I thank the Lord, the angels, and most of all Mam and Dad.

The next morning, I go to the bank and arrange the mortgage. I am accepted. I am told that I need to put in a 30 per cent deposit because it is a business mortgage. I inform my solicitor and begin the searches for the sale. Three months later, the probate has cleared, and I am the proud owner of a shop and flat. Now I just have to tell Roger. He is going to hit the roof!

I get home that evening, and Roger tells me that he has booked us a weekend in Edinburgh for my fortieth birthday next weekend. He asks if the will has been sorted yet and how much I think I will get. I reply, "No, I don't know." He adds that he has seen a nice flat that we could buy. I decide that this is not the right time to tell him my news; I will wait until next weekend.

Lorna, Sophie, and Andy know about my new purchase and have all been sworn to secrecy. The next day, I tell them all about Roger's surprise, and how I have decided to tell him about the shop when we go away. They think I am mad because Roger will hit the roof! I reply that if he leaves me, he leaves. I am not bothered anymore.

As the weekend approaches, I make arrangements with the children for when I am away, and I tell them to ring Sophie if they need anything. I leave money and supplies for the boys at Dad's house. Polly is staying at the house with her boyfriend to mind the dogs.

Roger and Polly have not been getting on. He complains about her boyfriend eating all his food, and it is embarrassing her. I have arranged with Lorna that if the shit hits the fan when I tell Roger, she is to go get the animals and Polly and take them up to my father's, where they will be safe. I am taking some money and have stashed it away, just in case he leaves me there, so I can catch the train home.

Saturday morning arrives, and we leave for Edinburgh. On the journey, Roger comments on how quiet I am. Little does he know I am panicking and dreading the next few days.

When we arrive, he tells me to book in, and he will park the Land Rover to which he has treated himself (it is not brand-new). I go to the check-in desk and am struggling with the bags; Roger is not a gentleman. I get to the counter and give the lady my name. She is foreign and tells me in broken English that I have room number 666, and the porter will take me to my room. I am speechless and do not want this room.

The porter is also foreign and is a little man. As he ushers me into the lift, he looks at my room number and keeps repeating like an little elf, "Ha-ha, you have room 666!" I tell him to fuck off.

I get into my room and ring Lorna. I tell her my room number and say that it's a bad omen – I am jinxed. She cannot stop laughing. Eventually, she asks if I am OK. I reassure her but add I am nervous. I tell her that I have to speak to Roger tonight – I cannot leave it any longer. She wishes me luck, and I end the call as he enters the room.

I comment on the room number, and Roger tells me it doesn't bother him because he is not religious. I remind him that I am a Catholic. He tells me that we are going out for an Indian tonight, his treat. Within an hour, we have showered, changed, and found a restaurant. I decide to wait until the meal is over; I am hungry and want to eat first. We order a bottle of wine, and the food is not very good. I pick at my meal, and eventually I pluck up the courage and decide it is time to spill the beans.

I start by telling Roger I want to talk. I ask him to listen to me and give me ten minutes of his time, because I have something to tell him. (He always shouts me down in an argument, and I can never get my point over.) He agrees that he will not interrupt.

I blurt out, "I have used my inheritance to buy a shop and flat. I want the flat for the boys, because I am worried that they will have nowhere to live if my father's house sells. I know you won't have them back home, and they do not want to live with you either." I tell him that the running costs of the shop will be cheaper, and it is a great location. "I have looked into getting a grant on the property, and I should qualify."

He nearly chokes and answers, "What! You said we would buy a flat for us to rent out!"

I reply, "No, that is what *you* wanted."

He shouts back that telling him that the flat was for the boys is like a knife in his back.

He tells me to get up because we are leaving. I try to reason with him all the way back to the room. He tells me that I have killed the marriage and betrayed him. At this point, I don't care anymore, but I am worried that he might beat me up. When we get back to the room, I stay in the chair all night and only go to the bed when he is snoring. The next day, Roger tells me to pack my bags because we are heading home. I text Lorna to tell her we are on our way back, and that I am OK.

The next month is spent in silence. Roger ignores me; the only comfort I have is Benji. Roger feeds him liver and raw eggs to build him up, and he farts a lot! Benji always lies with his head on my lap and farts all over Roger. I kiss his face and tell him I love him, and he is my boy.

After three weeks of being ignored and given evil glares, I decide I have had enough. Each morning after Roger goes to work, I start packing up my most precious possessions: my photos and things that I can never replace. I am not materialistic; I can replace every stick of furniture and jewellery. I pack them into the car and store them in Dad's house.

Eligh notices and asks, "Are you leaving him?" I reply that I am, and it is time to go. He asks when, and I tell him it will be soon.

I get home the following Saturday evening. Roger is drinking, and he speaks for the first time in weeks, saying he has bought tickets for the Social Club. There is a band playing tonight called the Skanks, and he thought it would do us good to go out. I have dropped Polly at her boyfriend's, and he has agreed to walk her home by eleven. I use this as my excuse and tell him that Polly doesn't like coming into an empty house, so I won't bother. I tell him to go out with his mates instead. I walk into the bedroom to shower and change into my pyjamas.

He pushes me onto the bed, holding my arms over my head, and tells me he has decided that I can have the shop, but he wants an extra hundred pounds a week off me. He adds that he is not going to help me do any repairs or refurbishing; I can do it myself. Does he expect me to thank him or be pleased? I think to myself, *Fuck you!*

He tells me to get ready because we are going out – he is not going to take no for an answer. He thinks that he has won and have agreed to his demands. Eventually, I tell him to go on over, and for once he does, but he adds I should hurry up. I ring Lorna and tell her what has happened. She tells me she is working nights, and if I need her, I can ring her. I thank her and tell her I will.

As I walk over to the Club, I pray to God, the angels, and Mam and Dad. I ask them to help me through this. I look over at the mountain: the sun is setting, and through a cloud, I see a beam of light. I take this as a sign, and it gives me hope.

I enter the Club, see my friends, and sit down. Roger is drunk. Throughout the night, he starts giving me stinking looks. My friends notice and tell me that they don't think I should go home tonight. They offer for me to stay at their place. I thank them and accept the offer. Five minutes later, Roger sits next to me and says, "Get your fucking coat. We are going home – and when we get there, I am going to fucking kill you."

I calmly reply, "Well, I am not going home, then." I am not afraid of him, and I never have been.

He replies, "Polly is in the house." I look at the time: it is after eleven. I am scared and pick up my phone to call her, but he grabs my hand and pushes me onto the seat. His mates grab him and pull him off me. He soon storms out of the club. The phone is ringing, and Polly answers. I ask her where she is, and she apologises and says that she is running late and is still on her way home. I tell her to hide around the corner, because Roger has flipped out. I will come and get her.

Twenty minutes later, Polly and I are safe in my friends' flat, drinking a cup of tea. Polly is telling them that she is so proud of me. She thought I would never leave him. We all laugh. My marriage is over!

The next morning, I wake early and text Lorna to pick us up. Polly is awake and whispering about how flat the pillows are, adding hers is like tissue paper. We dress and go to the bottom of the road, where Lorna has arranged to pick us up. When she arrives I tell her that I want to go pick up my car, because he is not keeping it. Lorna reluctantly drives me to the house. I look through the window and realise that he hasn't gone home either. I go to the car and tell Polly and

Lorna we should go in and let out the dogs. I pick up my car keys and tell Lorna to help me pack up my clothes. Polly has gone to her room to get what she can carry.

Ten minutes later, Roger arrives. He looks like crap and tells me we need to talk. I decline his offer and tell him I am going up my father's house. I need a few days to think about what I want to do.

As I enter the bedroom, I notice that Lorna is packing my clothes in record time. Roger comments, "It doesn't look like it's only for a couple of days." Lorna acknowledges him with a nod and carries on packing. I look into my wardrobe: she has stripped it bear and hasn't left so much as a thong! I am impressed and try not to laugh. She goes upstairs and helps Polly. I can see that Roger is getting flustered, and I call to them and tell them we are leaving now. They take the hint and come downstairs with pillows and boxes.

As we leave, I look at Lorna and comment, "Argh, what about the dogs?"

She replies, "Where the fuck are we going to put them?" I turn and look at our cars. She has filled them to the brim. We burst out laughing.

Roger is coming up the steps and shouting that we need to talk. We decide it's time to get in the cars and leave.

A Fresh Start

When we get to Dad's, we empty the cars, and Lorna heads home. I break the news to Sophie and Andy. They laugh about the day's events and offer to help me unpack. I tell Sophie, "It feels like the stress has been lifted from my shoulders." I have a day off tomorrow and intend to have the first lie-in I've had in years!

The children are happy. I am relieved it is all over and that we are a proper family again. Friday nights become our cinema night. We have takeaway and a film, and it is great, like the old days. I have my family back.

After flowers, cards, and loads of text messages and voicemails, I agree to meet Roger to talk about the details of the divorce. I am only asking for the savings of £10,000 and my £55,000 that I paid off his mortgage. This is more than fair, and he knows it.

We meet at a local pub, and he suggests going for a meal, adding that I owe him that much. I agree and want to keep it on friendly terms. We order the meal, and as we are talking, he grabs my hand. When I look up, he is crying. He tells me that he will buy the boys a house to live in and will do anything to have me back. He tells me that Benji is pining for me, sits by the window, and cries for me all the time. I ask him if, after the meal, I can go to see Benji and make sure he is OK. He agrees.

As I enter the house, Benji jumps up on my lap. I catch and kiss him, telling him I love and miss him so much. I sit there for an hour with him, and will not move off my lap. He even cries when I go to the toilet, thinking I am going to leave. I stay longer than I intended, and it is late. Roger tells me to stay the night and pours me a glass of wine. We talk and end up having drunk make-up sex.

The next morning, I get up early, make my excuses, and leave. I kiss Benji goodbye and tell him I love him. As I go through the gate, he starts to cry. Leaving him is so hard, but I know I cannot take him with me, because he is offically Rogers. I get in the car and drive back to my father's house. Roger thinks we are back together. I am gutted and know I have made a massive mistake. When I get in, Lorna and the children are waiting. Jonah tells me, "Mam, we need to talk."

Lorna told them that I was going to talk to Roger, and they tell me they were worried. Lorna adds that she knows what Roger is like and how manipulative he can be. I tell them that I am OK and am not going back to him. Jonah says, "Mam, I know you are confused and on your own right now, but you are only forty. That is not old. Maybe it won't be right now, but in a few years, you will meet someone else. You won't be on your own forever."

Polly adds, "If you go back to him, he will have what he has always wanted: you without us." She adds that she is not going back there ever, and that I can have him, but then I won't have them. I tell them they are right, and I promise them that I won't go back. My mind is made up.

The next day, I tell Sophie what has happened, and she says that at least now I know. Maybe going back and trying to make it work was what I needed to do, to get it out of my system. I text Roger and tell him that it is definitely over. He leaves several disgusting messages, accusing me of being a slag and telling me that no one has ever hurt him this much. Deep down, I know he is more hurt over losing the lifestyle we had, and he doesn't want to repay me my money.

As the months pass and the solicitors' letters change hands, Roger becomes bitter. He tells me that he intends to drag the divorce out for as long as possible. I get a text from Roger that reads, "By the way, the dog is dead." I call him and ask what is he on about. He tells me Benji had a problem with his leg, and the pet insurance covered the cost of the surgery, but he died on the table. I had been visiting him when I knew that Roger would be at work. I tell him that he is lying and hang up. I am at work, and Ali is also in today. I ask her to cover my clients for an hour because I have to pop out.

I drive to the house to look for Benji. He is not in the garden. I look in through the kitchen window, and his cage is empty.

I leave the house and drive to a local park because I need to be alone. I start to cry for Benji, Mam, and Dad. I can't stop and sob my heart out. About an hour later, I am cried out and have a thumping headache. I ring Lorna and tell her about the dog, and I start crying all over again. I tell her, "I couldn't cry when we lost our parents, so why am I crying over a dog?" She reminds what I have been through the last five years and tells me that it will be OK.

I thank her for listening and hang up.

I am crying again, and this time I pray to God. "Please don't let me break." I lie in bed that night and think about Roger and how he told me about Benji. He could have let me say goodbye.

The next day, I go get a tattoo on my hip. I choose a fairy, and she has swirls around her. I tell him to add a cute bumblebee. The *B* is for Benji.

A month later, when I am at work, Ali comments that it has been on the news about breast implants, and that there has been a problem with a certain type used. I look at my paperwork and discover that I have PIP implants. I ring Harley Street and explain that my circumstances have changed financially, and I cannot afford to replace them. I also tell them I cannot afford to be ill. They recommend that I have private scan to check whether the implants are leaking. Although the scan is expensive, It puts my mind at rest luckily they are not.

Jonah has graduated from university with a 2.1 grade, and I am proud of him. Eligh has moved into a flat because he says that he wants to live on his own. I apply to the local council, and they offer him a one-bedroom flat in a four-storey building. I think letting him have a taste of the real world will do him good, but I help him by buying a sofa, carpets, and a bed. Lorna buys him a microwave and has an old fridge and freezer that she gives him. I visit him weekly and make sure he has enough money for food and electric. I worry that he is depressed and ask Jonah to keep an eye on him. Jonah tells me that he will; he is the only one who can talk to Eligh these days.

Jonah has asked Eligh if he can film some scenes for his new documentary and sitcom series that he is making at his flat, and Eligh agrees. The other locations for the series are my shop, the flat, and Dad's house (our new home). He has asked if the crew can stay at the house for a week, and I agree. The day before they all arrive, he informs me that I will also have to cater for two vegans! Jonah has co-written the series with his gay best friend, Tim. They have become great friends and work partners since meeting in university. Polly is devastated that Jonah has a gay friend and she doesn't. Tim tells her that he will be hers as well, and Polly is overjoyed.

The week of filming is a great experience. Eligh and Frankie assist everyone and have a good laugh with all the actors and film crew. Everyone has sleeping bags and crash in the living room. Jonah is a great cook and helps me prepare all the meals. I do my speciality, a cauliflower cheese dish for the vegans, and they love it. Jonah and Tim finish filming, and the crew and actors thank me for my hospitality before leaving. I realise that I would never have been allowed to be involved in that experience if I were still married to Roger.

Six months later, Eligh is struggling to cope in the flat. He cannot get a job. He comes to the house most days to eat, and he looks skinny and depressed. I ask how things are going, and he tells me that he is finding it hard to cope. I tell him to come home, he sighs and then agrees.

I have been successful in obtaining the grant for refurbishment at the new premises. I am struggling financially and am stressed. Roger lives in the house mortgage-free. I tell him I want the furniture that I took there from my old house: the children's beds and bedroom furniture, kitchen utensils, and ornaments. I ask for the Halifax savings (my teaching money pay). I also want my £55,000 that I paid off his mortgage. I remind him that my name is on the deeds to the house. We have had the house valued, and it is worth £180,000. Roger has a good job and no dept thanks to me. I tell him that he could get a mortgage on the house and easily pay me back. We could be divorced in four months if he would only see sense. He offers me £25,000. I tell him to piss off.

Roger knows that I need the money to pay towards the grant I have obtained on the shop and flat, but he is determined to drag out the divorce. I am on my knees financially, and eventually I manage to make arrangements with the builder to pay him in instalments. I change my car. The garage I deal with is trustworthy and gives me three thousand back for the Audi and an older model Audi. I use the money to pay my first instalment.

Three months later, I finally convince Roger to split the Halifax savings. He only does this because I have the book, and he is afraid I will get the money out. I cannot do this because we have to co-sign (I have tried). I use the five thousand to pay the builder the second instalment. Six months later, I persuade Sophie and Lorna to get a mortgage on Dad's house. Andy wants to be bought out. We need to add a new bathroom and windows to the house to get it into a rentable condition. The money that is left from the mortgage after this is split three ways. I use my share to pay a third instalment to the builder. I have to scrimp and save every spare penny to pay him. He is hard work and is adding extra costs to the refurbishment.

Eventually, eight months later, I tell him to give me the final balance. I have been making him sign a receipt every time I give him money. I add up the total amount I have already paid him, and we conclude that the balance owing is two thousand. I get a loan to pay him off and tell him that this is his last payment. I am broke and at breaking point.

Roger instructs his solicitor to go for my shop and my inheritance. This is the final straw. He has told his solicitor that he has paid to decorate my old premises and is owed money. He is such a fucking liar! He drags the divorce out for two years. When it is finalised, I get my furniture, £55,000, and the caravan. I have had £5,000 of the Halifax savings. Oh, yes, and a bill from my solicitor for £6,500. Cheers!

Polly has been great since the divorce, often working for free to help me out. None of us has had new clothes or shoes for ages. I am still struggling to make ends meet, and I tell them all that I will make it up to them. Polly has become more than a daughter; she is a good friend. She and Jonah have been my private counsellors. I pay back Lorna and Sophie what I owe them, and I am left with £41,500. I sold the caravan for £6,500; this is included. It was worth twice that, but I wanted a quick sale.) The house that I wanted to buy a year ago is still on the market. I put in an offer, and with the help of an excellent financial advisor, I manage to get a mortgage. It means that I have to put down a deposit of £30,000, but the house is mine. It is in a private location and is an old property that has a cottage feel to it, with its original, solid-wood latch doors throughout and painted wooden beams on the living room ceiling.

Before we move in, I have to have it rewired throughout. A new bathroom suite is put in and tiled floor to ceiling, along with a power shower. I also have an attic conversion done. I need an extra bedroom for Polly. The three bedrooms I have are small. I take the front one, and Jonah has the box room. Eligh and Frankie share a room. It is a squeeze, but we all fit in and are a family in our home.

Surprisingly, after all that I still manage to have enough left over for a holiday. I get passports for Eligh and Frankie because the old ones have expired. Jonah had one whilst in university; he needed it for ID when hiring out the cameras to film his work. I pay for us all to go to Kos in Greece, and I include a ticket for Jack (Polly's boyfriend) and Carla (Jonah's girlfriend).

A month later, we head to the airport. This is the first family holiday we have had together since before the move to Roger's. We land in Kos, and the resort is run by a friendly family. The owner introduces himself as George.

When we arrive, we are shown to our rooms. Jack, Polly, and I share a room. Eligh and Frankie are next door, and Jonah and Carla are the other side of us. Later that evening, we walk into town for food and drinks. On the way, we spot a bike hire shop, and the next day we decide to hire some push bikes. Eligh has been quite moody with me since I came back to live at Dad's. He has never said it, but I don't think he has been able to forgive me for making him put up with Roger. Jonah and Carla are good with him. Despite this, the next day Eligh tells us that he does not want to go to the beach, and he says to go without him. Jonah tells me to leave him in the room. we shout to him that he knows where we are if he changes his mind, and then we leave.

Carla decides that the roads are too busy and is too nervous to get a bike. I tell her that there are bicycle lanes all over the island, but she declines.

The rest of us get mountain bikes with baskets on the front. They have keys to lock them, and we hire one each for the week. We cycle to the beach. It is sectioned off into strips, and we pick one that has a mixture of age groups sunbathing on it. It has eighties music playing in the background. Jonah says, "This is the place for us!" He loves this music. We order drinks. There is an eighteen to thirty section, where they are having drinking games.

Later in the day, we have lunch on the beach and more drinks. I worry about Eligh, and Jonah and I comment that it is not the same without him. As we cycle back to the resort, we see him. Eligh says that he has been down at the beach several times looking for us, but he couldn't find us. We tell him that he missed out on a great day. After that, Eligh gets up in the mornings and joins in. Jonah has a personality that attracts people to him, and before the second day is out, he is friends with the whole family at the resort, as well as everyone staying there.

Carla argues with Jonah for most of the holiday. I notice that she can be quite moody, and she spends most of the holiday chatting to Eligh. I am glad he has come out of his shell and is making an effort to get to know her for Jonah's sake. It is the first holiday where I have made friends. Jonah tells me that John (his new friend) commented that I do not mix with anyone. After meeting him and his wife, I explain to them that taking my children away on my own for so many years has been hard, and no one has ever tried to mix with us, so I have learned to keep myself to myself. I apologise to them both and tell them I was not being ignorant.

I am the only one out of us who goes to bed before 2.00 a.m. most mornings. The kids, their partners, and the rest of the resort stay up playing pool. I notice that Eligh is like a different person here: he is witty and funny, has a laugh, and joins in with everyone. By the end of the week, we are all gutted and do not want to leave. We have farewell drinks with the resort owners and the other guests, and we promise to keep in touch on Facebook. We all agree this was the best holiday ever!

Three months after the holiday, Carla and Jonah split up. Jonah tells me that she was seeing someone else. He is upset and asks me to pick him up from work so that we can talk about it in private. I joke that people will think we are a courting couple, but I pick him up as requested. I park the car, and he tells me everything. He decides that it is for the best.

Three weeks later, Carla is on the phone, telling him she wants him back and it is all off with the other bloke. I advise Jonah that it is his decision, but if he goes back, then he will never trust her again. I tell him about what happened early on with me and Roger, and I reveal to him that I never really trusted him after that. Jonah tells me he does not want to have a relationship with no trust and that they always said neither of them would cheat; if one did, it would be the end of the relationship. He texts Carla and tells her that he does not want her back.

A month later, he is on the Plenty of Fish website looking for dates! I did not get divorced to be single again. The thought of dating at my age makes me cringe. Roger, as I predicted, has moved in his new girlfriend. Over the last two years, he has had several and cannot be on his own. My friends tell me that she is a supervisor in a factory and earns good money. That is all that matters to him, and the first thing he tells people is not that she is nice, pretty, or even slim, but that she earns a good wage. It sums him up.

Since splitting from Roger, I have moved four times. Until then, I didn't realise how much crap I hoarded. I moved from Roger's to my father's, and then from there to the flat. This was just Polly and I, because we had to speed up the builders who were taking forever to complete the work. I moved back from the flat to Dad's and eventually from there to my new home.

On a night out, my friends jokingly ask, "which residence would you like to go home to tonight Lauren Sugar?" This is their nickname for me because they joke that am a property tycoon. I own a third share in my parents' house, which we are now renting out. I own a shop with a flat above and also my new home. This means I have three mortgages to pay.

I jokingly reply, "The new residence, please, and make it snappy."

Apart from the occasional night out with the girls, I spend most of my spare time and money doing up the new house. Each room is replastered (including the ceilings) and redecorated. I finish the kids' bedrooms. I also strip the paint from ceiling beams in the living room, the fireplace, and the landing and stairs; it is all adjoined. The staircase is neat and opens up into the room. This has taken months of hard work. I stain the beams and the staircase and am proud of the job I have done.

Six months later, I have saved and have just enough to buy and fit a new kitchen with a Harga cooker. I paint the whole downstairs and tile the kitchen and dining room. I have bought second-hand furniture to match the theme of the house. I love the results. It is nearly Christmas, and I buy a new Christmas tree. It looks great in the newly finished living room.

I have invited Lorna and her husband for Christmas dinner, along with Polly's boyfriend Jack. Polly and Jack have been together for three years. A month before Christmas, Jonah gets a new job and has moved to the city with his new girlfriend, Laura; they are also coming for dinner. We have the best Christmas ever, and I cook it to perfection. I have a dishwasher in my new kitchen. After lunch, we load it, turn it on, and go watch a film. Life is good, we are a proper family again, and I love our new home. The house is not quite finished, but I am broke and plan to save up next year to complete it.

In January, it is my friend's fortieth birthday, and although I am broke, I agree that Polly and I will go out for the birthday celebrations. She has booked rooms, and we are staying overnight in the Ibis. Polly tells me it will do me good to get out and to stop worrying about money. Polly and I arrive later than the rest of the group because we have to work Saturdays. We meet them in Wetherspoons before heading to the hotel to pre-drink and get ready. We have a colour scheme of pink and black; it is quite hard to find anything pink in winter.

I wear my old, faithful black dress. Polly looks great; she wears a plum dress and tells me that it will have to do, and bugger the colour scheme. We are kitted out in butterfly wings and pink boas, and we head into the city centre. The birthday girl has several "I am 40 today" balloons and banners attached. I tell the girls that the balloons are so we can track her down – she has a tendency to wander. We burst into laughter. We head to a pub on the other side of town that has great bands playing every night. My friend Josie is out with us. She lives alone with her daughter, and she tells me on the way to the pub that she is glad that we are heading there, because it is a great atmosphere and the drinks are cheap. I laugh and agree with her. We enter the pub, trying not to bash anyone with our matching butterfly wings.

I spot a nice-looking bloke smiling at us. I assume that it is because of the costumes, and that he is with the lady next to him. An hour later, I notice that he is on his own. I have had a drink, and so when he smiles at me, after a nudge from Polly I walk over to say hello. The music is loud, and I have a job to hear him. I tell him that I am out with my daughter, and he introduces himself to Polly. He tells me that he thinks that it is great that we have such a good relationship. I instantly like him, and I tell him over the loud music that I detect an accent and ask him where he is from. He tells me he is Australian, and his name is Drew.

When it is time to move onto the next pub, I tell Drew to come with us. He is on his own, is over here on a business trip, and is divorced. He tells me that he will be here for two weeks and will be travelling around the country. Polly asks him about the sharks, spiders, and kangaroos in Australia, and he laughs at her.

We go to the next pub, and the DJ is playing seventies and eighties music. We dance all night. Polly is chatting to the DJ and wearing a pink feather boa around her neck. We watch her and laugh because he is letting her choose all the songs. Drew tells me I am beautiful, I love his accent. He hugs me close and then runs his hands down my body. Then he picks me up off the floor and pulls me close to him, as if I am as light as a feather. I am impressed – Drew is strong as an ox.

The girls have all gone for food. It is late, so Polly, Drew, and I head back to the hotel. Polly is drunk and asks the taxi driver if he can stop at Burger King. He starts protesting. Polly is disgusted and tells him, "That is no way to speak to a customer. It is not good customer service." I remind Polly that he has been working all night and is tired, and she should not cheek her elders. She is not happy.

We get back to the hotel, and I apologise to Drew for her behaviour. He replies, "No worries. She's drunk – and hungry." We laugh. Polly is annoyed with me, and she tells me that she is bunking up with Josie tonight; I can sleep on my own. Josie tells me not to worry because she will be OK in the morning, and Josie will watch her. Drew looks at me and says, "Come on. Let's go back to mine." He is staying at the Hilton.

The next morning, we chat and snuggle up – something we both admit we miss more than sex. I tell him that we call snuggling up a cwtch here. He tries to say it with his accent, but it sounds funny, and we laugh. We shower together, and he takes me back to my hotel. Polly is packing up her stuff and says hi to us both. Drew asks if she is feeling better, and she replies, "A bit." He chats to the girls as I pack up and change. I go outside to say goodbye to him and tell him that I can't believe I won't see him ever again.

He asks for my number and rings my phone. I log his number into mine, and he explains that he has had to buy a new phone here because his network doesn't work. We kiss, and he tells me he will try his best to get back and see me before he goes home. We say goodbye, and the girls and I head to the train station. They all tell me that he is a lovely bloke, commenting that it's a shame he lives in Australia.

Two days later, I am at work, and my phone rings; it is Drew. I go into the office for privacy and answer the phone. He asks how I am and struggles to understand my strong accent. I tell him that I am OK and ask how he is, and what part of the country is he in. He tells me that he is on his way back to my village. I offer to cook him dinner at mine; I have already made some pies this morning before work. I explain to Drew that he will not be able to stay at my home, out of respect for my children. He agrees and books a nearby hotel.

Around six thirty, Lorna arrives just before Drew. She stays and chats to him as I complete the finishing touches to the food. Then she leaves before I dish up. Frankie is in the living room, and Drew tells him he is lucky to have a mam who is hard working like me; Frankie smiles and agrees. Polly says hi, makes her excuses, and heads to Jack's.

After the meal, we chat over a glass of wine. Drew tells me all about Australia, where he is from, his children, and how they live out there. He tells me about the beautiful beaches and his horses; he has a small holding and three horses, and he rides every day. Later, we say goodnight to Frankie. I tell him I will be back in the morning, and we head to Drew's hotel. It is not as plush as the Hilton, but it has a bed and a shower, and that is all we need.

Drew has a hypnotic accent, and I listen to him talk for hours before nodding off into a deep sleep. Morning comes too fast. I have to go to work, and he is due in Manchester in four hours for a meeting with work. We shower and kiss goodbye. He tells me that he will try to make it back to me before he leaves, and we kiss again. As I turn to leave, he slaps me on the arse and says, "Bye, beautiful."

I go to the house. Polly is there, tapping her fingers on her arm and jokingly asking me, "Where have you been? You're a dirty stop out!" we laugh and head for work. It is a Tuesday. Tuesdays and Wednesdays are our OAP days. We have regular customers who have been coming for their shampoo and sets for years. This is very often their only time out of the house, and they enjoy the company and chat to each other every week. Lilly is due in today; Polly has nicknamed her the Penguin because she waddles when she walks. Polly is also a little scared of her, saying that she stares at her all the time. I explain that she is harmless and simply likes her. Polly tries her best to avoid shampooing her. Today, Lilly has rang to tell me she will be a little late because she is at the dentist. I tell her to come in when she can.

Another regular customer is Ethel. She comes in every fortnight for her shampoo and set. Ethel has very fine hair and sprays it with hairspray to hold it in place. After two weeks of excessive spraying, it is like a crash helmet. She arrives on time, and as routine, Polly passes her the brush so that she can crack the shell of hairspray. She then proceeds to brush it out, causing a snow storm. Polly offers Ethel a cup of tea; this is her excuse to avoid being covered in crustations. Polly shampoos Ethel, and I set her and put her under the dryer with her cup of tea.

Then before Polly can hide in the office, Lilly enters. I turn to say hello and notice that she has had her new teeth fitted. My first thought is that it looks like someone has thrown a radiator into her mouth. She is trying to close her lips and staring at me. I stifle a laugh and pretend that is a cough. As I turn around, I see Polly slipping into the office, and her shoulders are shaking. I bite my cheek to avoid giggling and ask Lilly to come to the basin. I shampoo Lilly, I have to do this with her standing over the basin because she cannot lean back far enough when sat down and ends up getting soaked. I do not want to offend her, and so I do not mention her new teeth.

I move her into the stylist's chair and offer her a cup of tea. She declines, so I carry on setting her hair. Lilly says, "Have you noticed something? I have new teeth."

I reply without looking up, "Oh, yes, I can see now." I tell her they are nice.

She says, "They are a bit big."

I say, "Yes, now you come to mention it, they do look big." As I glance up, she is still trying to close her mouth. It is never going to happen, and I wonder how many calories she is burning by trying to hold them in her mouth! What has that dentist done to her?

Lilly as always asks after Polly, and she says, "She's a pretty girl."

I feel sorry for her and tell her she should go back to the dentist if she is not happy with her new dentures. Before Lilly leaves, Ethel is ready to come from under the dryer. Ethel and Lilly chat while I back comb and strategically place every strand of Ethel's hair into place (there are not many). I back comb the crown of her hair forwards to create a fringe, as instructed by Ethel. Lilly books in for next week, says bye to everyone, and leaves the shop.

I finish Ethel's hair and watch as she reapplies her pale pink lipstick. Her mouth is shaped in an oval shape as she says, "Ain't that Lilly ugly?"

I am gobsmacked and wonder, *Just what does she see in that mirror?* Ethel looks like Skeletor with a bird's nest on his head! When Ethel leaves, I ask Polly if she noticed Lilly's new teeth. She turns away and then spins back around, her lips curled around her teeth. While staring into my face, she says, "Are you all right, Lauren?" We are in hysterics! Thirty minutes later, we are still laughing and my ribs are aching.

I finish work and head to the gym. I usually go there every morning, but didn't have time because I was with Drew. When I leave, I check my phone, and there is a text from him. Yes! I have been watching my phone all day. I am playing it cool and am determined that I am not going to scare him off. Usually if I want something, I fight for it. I like getting my own way, and I am stubborn and determined. I have learned the hard way that men like to make the first move. I open the text, and it reads, "I am sat in a restaurant and enjoying a glass of red wine and an amazing meal. The only thing that is missing is you!" I text him back and tell him I am just leaving the gym and am thinking of him too; he has been on my mind all day.

I am covering maternity leave in my teaching job and now work three days a week. I offered to cover, thinking that I would be teaching NVQ level one hairdressing. I was soon to discover that I would be teaching Comms, ICT, and AON level one qualifications. Training for this amounted to a day shadowing a heavily pregnant, stressed-out tutor. I did not have a clue what I had to teach, so I decided the best way would be to set the learner's work from an example copy of a passed qualification in each subject. I was instructed by my lead IV assessor (she assesses my work) that this would be OK, and because she was also new to her new role, we would have to learn on the job – literally! I have a full-time stylist and Polly working in the shop. I work six days a week, and along with the marking I do in the evenings, it is exhausting.

It has been three days, and Drew has texted me every day. I have replied to his texts, but I am still playing it cool. As I get in from a stressful day of teaching, Drew rings and tells me he is on his way back. I arrange to meet him in the hotel bar. We go for a meal and head back to his room. I tell him everything about my job and how my IV keeps changing the work after I have managed to get the learners to achieve it.

Drew tells me to hang in there and not worry. He gives me good advice on how to deal with the situation. I can talk to him about anything and love listening to his stories about where he has been and his adventures. He tells me about all the different countries he has visited.

Drew visits me one more time before he has to leave. It is sad, and in the morning he hugs (cwtches) me tight and tells me to look after myself. We exchange addresses and emails, and he promises to keep in touch with me, telling me he will email me when he gets home. As I drive to work that morning, I cannot stop crying. I pull over to try and compose myself. I cannot believe I will never see him again. I text him, saying, "Trust me! I finally find my soul mate, and he lives over the other side of the world." I press send, wipe my tears, and sort myself out. I have to go to work.

As I enter the classroom, my phone rings, and it is Drew. I excuse myself and answer the phone. He tells me he is at the airport and that he will miss me. He asks me to remember the good times we had and to not be sad. He tells me to look back on the memories and laugh about it. I reply that I will and tell him to have a safe journey. He tells me I am beautiful and that as soon as he gets home, he will email me.

A week later, as promised, I receive an email from Drew. He tells me that he has arrived home safely and has been riding his beloved horses. He sends me a picture of the view from his property; it is at sunset, and it's beautiful. I ask him if he will send a picture of a kangaroo for Polly. He replies that next time he sees one, he will. A week later, he has a picture of one on a football field; he calls it an oval. I tell him I love the fact that it is so bright and sunny over there, and he replies that the one thing he could not handle about living in my country is the rain. He states that he can understand how there are such high suicide rates over there, because it is so depressing. I agree and tell him that there are also no jobs for the youngsters. Drew replies that for those who want it, there are plenty of jobs in Australia, as well as apprenticeship opportunities. I think about how different life would be for me and my children if we lived there, and I mention it to Polly. She says, "Mam, come on. Let's move to Australia!"

The next day, I ask Eligh and Frankie if they would like to live in Australia for a year and work there. They both reply, "OK, why not?" Later that day, I ring Jonah and ask him if he and his new girlfriend, Laura, would like to come. Jonah says he would and adds that Laura's friends have gone, and they said it was fantastic. I think about my age. If the children decided to settle there, I would be too old by then to emigrate. I look into the age limits online and email an agency called Migrate Me. I get a call back within an hour. The lady explains that the company helps people to emigrate. For a fee near two thousand pounds, which can be paid in monthly instalments, they arrange everything, including working visas and flights for family (which have to be paid for separately). The lady also informs me that it would take around eighteen months to complete the necessary paperwork. I tell her to sign me up and pay my first instalment. This is my new goal!

I admit this is very impulsive, and you are probably thinking that I am doing this so I can be with Drew, but this is not entirely the case. If in eighteen months, I go there and Drew wants to be part of my life, then that is great. But I have grown up over the years. I know there is no Mr Darcy or knight in shining armour. Drew is not going to sweep me off my feet and ride away with me. I am doing this for me, but most of all for my children. I want them to have the best opportunities life has to offer, and I know that it is not here in this country anymore.

I think of Polly. She only has a job because I employ her. This is how it works here. There is a recession, and the only young adults who are working have had to, like Jonah move to the city to find work. You can only afford to live there if you are flat sharing with someone because the rent is so expensive. It depends on whom you know, not what you know.

Eligh and Frankie have not been so lucky. They are both fed up with attending college rather than having to sign onto the dole. Eligh is so talented at art and design. He has eight GSCEs and has done several voluntary jobs to gain experience in shop and office work. He cannot get a job anywhere. Frankie has completed three years in college on a car mechanic course and has achieved a level three NVQ in this subject. He cannot get an apprenticeship anywhere and has had to resort to signing onto the dole. I think of Eligh and how depressed he has become. More job opportunities are available for both Eligh and Frankie in Australia. Polly has always wanted to travel.

Finally, I think of what I want. I have worked hard for the last fifteen years and want an easier life, a different life-work ratio. I have earned it, and this is my reason for emigrating. Drew has simply drawn my attention to a whole new adventure. I think back to when I was a young child, and I always wanted to go on one. This is it – better late than never!

Migrate Me informs me what is needed. First I need to get my qualifications photocopied and authenticated by a solicitor. Then I have to forward the documents to them. I do this, and once my appointed advisor receives them, she tells me that the best option for me is to opt for a skills test. She tells me that it is $350 for the technical part and $750 for the skills assessment. I sign up for a 0 per cent interest credit card and add the fee to it. This is getting expensive. She tells me that I need to pass this to qualify for a visa. The test is booked for six weeks time.

This is a big secret for me; I have decided to not tell anyone except the children for now. Polly and the boys are sworn to secrecy about the move. I tell them that I do not want to upset Lorna, Andy, and Sophie, and that I will tell them nearer the time. I also tell them that I do not want to tell my friends or customers, because I worry that they will go to another salon, and I cannot afford for this to happen.

Life goes on as normal. Polly and Jack's relationship comes to an end. She is relieved and has plans to start going out with her old school friends. This is the first time she has been single, and I tell her to be careful, but to enjoy herself.

Several weeks later, Frankie meets a girl on Facebook. He tells me her name is Penny, and she wants to meet me. I am honoured because this is the first girl he has brought home. I assume that he has known her for a few weeks at least. I meet her, and she seems a little young in her ways for eighteen years, but I say nothing. A week later, Frankie tells me that they are going for a night out and staying in a hotel overnight, because it is Frankie's best mate's twenty-first birthday. I ask Penny if she has ID to get into the pubs, and she tells me that she hasn't, but it will be OK because she won't need it. Later, I tell Frankie that she will need ID if she is going to the city to drink, or else she will not get served. Penny tells me that she hasn't got any and is not worried. They go and have to remain in the hotel room because Penny cannot get served. I ask Frankie if he minded missing his best mate's birthday, and he tells me it's OK. He is smitten!

Eligh, Polly, and I have noticed that Penny is a little controlling and cries if she does not get her own way. She wants Frankie to see her every day and expects me to drive them to her home each night. Frankie and Polly have started having driving lessons, and both pass their theory tests. Penny mentions that her mother has said that when Frankie passes his test, he can drive her car. I tell her that is very good of her, but he will not be able to afford insurance on a car with that sized engine. Penny insists; she knows best. A week later, I get a call from Penny, and she says that I can buy her mother's car for Frankie for two hundred pounds. I remind her that although it is a generous offer, he will not get insurance. She tells me that her mother said that he would, and it will be OK. I hang up the phone. I text Frankie and tell him that he will not be getting that car. The next day, Penny rings me in work to tell me that her mother is sending off the documents of the car to get them put into Frankie's name. I am fucking furious! However, for his sake, I take some deep breaths and calmly tell her that Frankie is *not* buying that car.

A week later, Penny texts me. "Frankie's car has run out of tax. If you don't move it within twenty-four hours, it will be towed away. By the way, it needs two new tyres, and the MOT has run out. Mam says you need to do this first." She adds that her uncle has a spare driveway and he can store the car on there. Oh, and she wants me to fetch the money for the car payment because her mam wants to go shopping! Frankie is practically living at her house, and this makes it hard to speak to him without her listening. I am starting to realise that she is a nutcase.

I decide the only way to get through to her is to stay calm. I text back, "It is not Frankie's car!"

Eligh does not show much emotion or say a lot these days, however, even he tells me, "You have to get Frankie from her. She is fucking crazy!" I tell Eligh I am trying, but if I go mad, it will only push him closer to her.

Over the next three weeks, we have to suffer Penny. If Frankie comes home, she is with him. When I am at work, they stay at the house, and Eligh is also there. When I get home, Eligh takes me into the kitchen and says, "Mam! You have to get Frankie away from her. She is crazy!" He says that as Frankie walked down the stairs earlier, she called him and said, "Frankie, do you want a fuck!" Eligh heard him reply OK, and ten minutes later, Frankie comes downstairs white as a ghost and rubbing cream in his arse! I ask him why he is rubbing cream in his arse! Eligh replies, "He burnt it on the light bulb when he was shagging her!" I am hysterical. He adds, "Mam, please get him from her!"

Penny's family is also crazy. I learn that her mother is waiting to go into hospital for a hernia operation. This is why she hasn't worked for fifteen years! Her stepdad is a heroin addict who rings an ambulance once a day to demand his morphine injections for his dicky stomach. Penny's sister is pregnant, and Penny informs me that her stepdad doesn't like her boyfriend and beats him up all the time. I tell Frankie that he had better not get her pregnant, and he tells me that he won't. I am relieved when I find evidence proving that he is taking his own precautions. The one person Frankie listens to and takes advice from is Jonah. I ring him and tell him I need him to talk some sense into him. Jonah texts him and invites them both to dinner the following Friday. I go because I am the designated driver.

I introduce Jonah and Laura to Penny, and we order takeaway and chat. Jonah starts to tell Penny about how Frankie was when he was little. He mentions a story about when Frankie was young, he would hide for hours at a time, and eventually I would get really worried about where he was.

Penny replies, "Oh, that was like me. When I was little, I went on a picnic at the ponds with my family. I was only three at the time, and I decided to hide under the picnic blanket. No one could find me. They called out the sniffer dogs and everything. Ten hours later, I shouted surprise and jumped from under the blanket!" We are all speechless.

I am imagining her parents trying to put the food onto the bump under the blanket and the food tipping over). I reply, "Oh, well, then." I don't know what else to say.

Laura starts chatting to Frankie and asks him whether he has seen his friends lately. Penny replies, "Oh, no, we don't like that crowd anymore." She continues to tell us how she has fallen out with all of them. Jonah and I exchange glances.

The following Thursday, I get home from work to find Eligh unhappy. He informs me that Frankie and the "cookie monster" have been in all day, arguing. He says she is so loud that he hasn't been able to watch the telly in peace. I shout up hello to them, and within five minutes, I hear Penny thudding down the stairs. She informs me that it is her birthday next week, and Frankie has bought her a new mobile on contract. I raise my eyebrows and tell her that he hasn't got one on contract himself, mainly because he cannot afford it.

Frankie enters the kitchen and confirms that they have been shopping today, so if a phone is delivered in the morning, I should not open it. He adds, "It's coming here because her stepdad doesn't want her to have a contract phone."

I reply, "Wait a minute. So you have a phone registered to *this address,* and the contract is in Frankie's name. To make matters worse, you have done it knowing that she is not allowed to have one?"

Frankie says, "Yes. It's OK, Mam. I am going to make the payments. It's only twenty-five pounds a month."

I am fuming and reply, "How dare you do that without my permission! This address will be blacklisted if the payments are missed. It is *not* happening. Don't open it, because the phone is going back."

Penny starts to cry and thuds upstairs. Three hours later, she is still howling. Frankie comes downstairs to try to reason with me. I tell him, "She can howl all she likes. It is *not* happening." He goes back upstairs. I ring Jonah and tell him, "Jon, you have to talk to him!"

The next morning, I get up and go to work. When I get home, the phone is left unopened on the chair. I open it, ring the company, and arrange to have it picked up from my work address the following day. I notice that the house is quiet, so I go upstairs. Frankie's bedroom door is open, and I pass it to go into my bedroom. As I sit on the bed, I notice a letter addressed to me in childlike handwriting. It is written by

Penny. She says Frankie has moved into her parents' house with her, and they will never come here again!

I email Drew and tell him a little about it. I ask him if he thinks have I gone too far. He tells me, "It will be all right. No worries!" I tell him I am distraught. Then I ring Jonah and Laura. Laura rings Penny and tries to reason with her, but Penny tells her to mind her own business because she isn't his sister-in-law. She adds that she and Frankie are getting engaged!

Jonah rings him, and Frankie is upset that everyone is against him. Jonah replies, "We are not. We just want the best for you."

The next day, I get a text off Frankie's best friend. It reads, "Hi, Lauren. I am worried about Frankie. Penny has stopped him from bothering with me and his other mates. I think a lot of him, and he deserves better than her." I text him back, telling him that I am trying to sort things out, and so is Jonah. I thank him for letting me know. He replies that it is no problem and asks me to let him know that Frankie's OK, because he is worried about him. He also adds that he has heard a lot of things about the family, and they are always in trouble with the police.

Jonah rings me back and tells me that he has managed to get Frankie to talk to me. I text Frankie and ask him to meet me for a chat, because we need to clear the air. He agrees, and I tell him I will be there in ten minutes.

I arrive outside Penny's house in record time and beep the horn. Frankie gets into the car. He asks if I want to speak to just him, or should Penny come along as well. I state I will speak to him on his own. He shouts to her that he will be about fifteen minutes.

I drive down the road and tell him that I am going to park and want him to listen to me for ten minutes. Then he can tell me what he wants to do. He agrees. I tell him he has two paths he can take. The first one is stay with her. I add that I have heard a lot of bad things about this family, and he knows better than anyone that I am not a snob and will talk to everyone the same. But this family are nutters. I tell him that her mission in life is to drop one or maybe two kids, and then she will expect him to look after them, and he will never be able to afford to give them anything. I tell him that I know that the stepdad deals and takes drugs. He beats up her sister's boyfriend, and it is only a matter of time until the man starts to hit Frankie.

I also add that if he is in the house when it gets raided, they will blame him, and before he knows it he will have a criminal record. Then will never be able to get a job. I add that worst-case scenario, he will get sent to prison. Then Penny will be "lonely" and start sleeping with someone else, and the stepdad will get away scot-free, whilst he will be getting his head pushed against the shower wall, and some thug will rape him. I tell him I can help him now. But if he goes down that path, I cannot help because it will be too late. I tell him that just before he is raped, his thoughts will be of this night, and he will be thinking, "Why didn't

I listen to my mother?" I add that he will never be the same person again.

I show him his best friend's text to me and tell him that everyone is worried about him. I add that the second path is he can come with me now. Fuck his clothes – I can replace them, but I cannot replace him. I will take him to Jonah's. He can come to Australia next year with all of us and have a good life. I tell him that he will eventually meet a nice girl, but Penny is *not* it!

Frankie replies, "Drive!"

On the way to Jonah's, I ring him and tell him I need him to put up Frankie for a week. He asks what's going on, and I tell him we are on our way. Forty-five minutes later, we arrive at Jonah and Laura's flat. They ask him if he is OK. He looks shattered and starts to sob. I am devastated and wonder whether I have done the right thing. Jonah tells him to go in with Laura, and we will go get KFC for them all. I ask Jonah how can he think of food right now, and he says, "I want to ask you what happened. Fill me in." I tell him everything and show him the best mate's texts. Jonah replies, "Jesus! Mam, that was fucking harsh!"

I tell him, "I agree it's worst-case scenario, but it could actually happen!" We get back to the flat, and Frankie says he is not hungry. Jonah tells me he will be OK and tells me to go home. Jonah also takes Frankie's phone off him. There are fifty-seven missed calls from Penny!

The next day, I ring Jonah and ask how he is. He tells me he is much better and adds that Frankie has told him he didn't know how to get out of the situation. I am so relieved. I get a text from Penny that reads, "I am going to smash up your house, car, shop, and face!" Charming.

A week later, she has made it her goal in life to abuse and threaten all of Frankie's friends on Facebook. He has seen her true colours and tells Jonah, "When she threatened Mam, that was the last straw, and I hate her for that."

A month has gone by since the psycho girlfriend. Facebook has a lot to answer for! I talk to Frankie about it, and he admits that he is glad he is away from her. He tells me that she threatened all his friends. He has had to block her on his phone and Facebook.

Polly has started dating a new fella who is in the army, and his name is Eric.

Work is as busy as ever, and with me doing three days teaching, it means that Ali, my stylist, has taken over most of my regulars. I have built up a good clientele over the last thirteen years. I do not need to pay for advertising anymore because I get new clients through word of mouth.

I get texts from Drew about once a month. I tell him about Frankie, and he tells me how his children are getting on and sends photos of all the different places he visits when he is travelling for his job. I tell him how beautiful the place looks, and how I cannot wait to go there. I think about what

I will be giving up here. I have a lot of good friends, but my parents are gone now, leaving me with only Sophie, Andy, and Lorna, as well as my nephew and two nieces. I have an uncle, aunty, and cousins here. I will be leaving about fifteen family members behind. I know Sophie has always wanted to go to Australia, and she will visit me. We have become closer over the last few years, and I decide to tell her my plans. She is happy for me and cannot wait to visit. I tell her not to tell Lorna because I do not want to upset her yet.

I have heard from the Migrate Me team, and I have to complete a photographic record of before, during, and after evidence of all the hair services I offer. I tell the clients it is for my CPD with my teaching job, and they all agree to help. My teaching job is hard work. The IV I have been appointed is dyslexic, and although I am all for equal opportunities, this is ridiculous! I cannot do a thing right, and I change the work as instructed by her, getting the learners to achieve it. Then she changes the criteria again! She is driving me insane.

I text Drew and ask for his advice. He tells me if he were there, he'd slap me on the arse and tell me to hang in there. I tell him she is a bitch. He replies, "One day the bitch may be gone, and someone like you will be running the show." I thank him for the good advice and tell him he always makes me smile, and I miss his cwtches.

Polly and Eric have been together for three months, and they are getting on really well. He is a nice, and so is his family. He is the eldest grandson and the golden boy. Polly is not enjoying working for me anymore and has decided that hairdressing is not for her. I tell her that she must complete her NVQ level two apprenticeship; then if she decides to change her career, I will support her.

A week later, I go into work, and Ali tells me that she is finishing. She has a new job in a clothes shop and is giving up hairdressing! She gives me two weeks' notice. I have no cover for the shop. Polly is a lifesaver and offers to hold the fort until I get another stylist or my maternity cover finishes.

Two months later, I book my skills test for my visa and have to go London to complete it. I work in the shop most days now because my maternity cover with my teaching job has ended, and I am only teaching one day a week. Polly has nearly finished her apprenticeship. She helps me in the shop most days now, and I am grateful. I have been offered government funding to complete a level five business and management diploma with a company called T2. It takes twelve to eighteen months to complete and would normally cost around six thousand pounds. I accept a place on the course, and it starts next week. The course will take twelve months to complete. I have just completed my CAVA qualification; This will cover my CPD for over a year. I have a gut feeling I will need both qualifications.

I applied for a personal protection insurance refund three months ago. Last month I was notified that I had qualified for a repayment. It is enough to have my implants changed; the cost is £2,800. I have received £2,240 and have saved hard to make up the shortfall. A month later, I go into hospital and have them replaced. This is a weight off my mind. I am told that I need two weeks off work. I take four days because I have no cover. I go on light duties and am careful not to overdo it, but I still need to earn money. Five weeks later, I go for my six-week post-op check-up. The doctor tells me he is pleased with the results, and so am I. I email Drew and send him a photo with my bra on. He is impressed!

I haven't dated much this year. I have been too busy and have decided that I do not want to mess anyone around. I haven't met anyone worth dating. The problem is I always end up comparing them to Drew, and there is no comparison. I also do not want to start a relationship and end up hurting someone when I tell him that I will be leaving the country!

Eligh keeps changing his mind and tells me he is seeing someone now, so he does not want to come away. I tell him he has to come even if it is for a holiday, and his girlfriend can come with us. He says that she doesn't want to, and there will be spiders under every toilet seat.
I reassure him that is not the case.

Polly and Eric arrive at the house the following weekend and announce that they want to get married. She tells me she is not pregnant, but Eric has been deployed to Portsmouth. If they get married, it means that she can live up there with him. Polly is like me: if she wants something, she wants it yesterday and she is very determined to get it. I like Eric; she could do a lot worse. I agree to the wedding, deciding that I would rather help her and be happy for them both than be upset and push her away. I know her, and she will do it anyway!

We have two months to plan a wedding. I ask her who is going to give her away, and whether she would like Jonah to do it. Polly says she wants me to give her away. She says that I have always been there for her, and she would like me to do it. I tell her I am proud of her, give her a cwtch, and tell her that I will be honoured! I text Drew and tell him. He replies that she is too young. I reply to him that she has to make her own mistakes; they are besotted with each other, and I know it will work out. I add that I have warned her to not have children yet, because I do not want to become a nan!

I go to London and complete the skills test for my visa. I have revised for three weeks. I have practical knowledge, but they have not made it clear what they want me to do, so I freshen up on all the terms and conditions and health and safety regulations. I also revise the NVQ level two and three books. The day of the test, I am so nervous. The lady tells me not to worry and explains that I will be video linked to a hairdressing professional who will ask me questions on practical skills. I'll also talk to an Australian assessor who will be listening in and recording the test.

An hour later, it is all over and my brain is fried. I ask her how she thinks I did, and she replies that I was a lot better than some of them and tells me not to worry. The following week, I am ill with my stomach, this time due to my healthy eating. I cannot keep anything in my stomach and I have to gradually reintroduce food. I eat a diet of white bread, rice, and boiled chicken. I still go to work because I have no cover. I know it is the stress of the course that has brought this on.

Two weeks later, I get the results of the skills test. I have passed! I forward my results to my Migrate Me adviser. She congratulates me and asks me if I have completed an IELTS test. I tell her I have done so much that I am not sure. She tells me to go online to check and adds that it costs £150. The next day I check and see that I have not completed it. She adds that I have to complete this before she can apply for my visa. I book the test. The next available date in my area is in six weeks' time, just after the wedding.

Polly looks stunning in her dress. We manage to pull together a beautiful wedding with the help of family and friends. The weather is warm and sunny, and we have a fantastic day. My daughter is a married woman. Two weeks later, she moves away with Eric. I sulk for the first weekend and miss my girl terribly. I only have Frankie and Eligh at home now, and they have their own friends and interests. I am happy that everyone has a social life, but it leaves me feeling sad and alone. I am lonelier than I have been in my whole life.

I text Drew and tell him how I am feeling. Although I wouldn't have it any other way for the children's sake, and I have a lot of family and friends, inside I feel alone. I confide that I don't tell anyone else how I feel because I don't want sympathy. I simply want help and advice of how to get through it. Drew understands, and I know he is the only one who does. He suggests a holiday and asks me to come out to visit Australia. I reply that maybe I will.

My teaching job has come to an end. The government funding in the schools has dried up, and therefore I am not needed. I and five other members of staff are made redundant. I did not realise that I would get redundancy pay, and although it is not a lot, it pays for my plane fare to Australia and a cheap car for Frankie. This is for his twenty-first birthday, and he has passed his test.

The day of my IELTS test arrive, and I am so nervous. The exam conditions are very strict. I have been revising for weeks online. I go into the room, and I am only allowed my ID, pens, and pencils. I am not allowed to talk to anyone or look around the room because the examiners will suspect me of cheating, and I will be removed from the exam and disqualified. I have the speaking test first, then the listening test. Next I complete the reading test, and last is the written test. I find writing the hardest. I complete the first part, but the subject I have to write about on the second is difficult. I go blank and the clock is ticking – I have forty minutes. When the test is finished, I am relieved and tell myself I have achieved it to the best of my ability. It takes two weeks to get the results.

My results come back, I have an overall score of 7.1 and a C1 grade. I text my Migrate Me advisor with my overall and separate scores. They are speaking 9.0, reading 7.0, writing 6.5, and listening 7.5. I am chuffed to bits and think I have passed. Two hours later, I get a message back saying that due to the fact I only have a 6.5 score on my writing, I will have to do it all again; as unfair as this sounds, the migration company needs me to score a 7.0 or above on all tests. I text back that I am gutted. I ring the IELTS centre, and although the lady is sympathetic, she tells me it is £60 for a remark. At least I will only have my written test remarked. The waiting time is eight weeks, just before I fly out to Australia for my holiday.

I go for the remark, pay for it, and await the results. I email Drew, telling him that I have booked a flight and giving the date I will be landing. I tell him I cannot wait to see him, and I want to visit different areas in Australia to decide where I want to settle. I have not had a holiday in over a year and am very excited to go. My friends and family think I am mad for travelling out there alone, but I cannot wait for my adventure.

I think about everything I have to sort out before I can emigrate. Three months ago, Sophie, Lorna, and I agreed to a sale price for Dad's house with the tenants. It should be finalised after I return from my holiday. After the mortgage and selling fees are paid off, we should be left with around seven thousand each. This money will pay for all the tickets and visas needed for all of us. Polly and Eric, along with Jonah and Laura, have agreed to come out for a month. Frankie, Eligh, and I are going for at least a year, and if we like it we will stay. I am hoping to convert them all eventually!

Last month, I had the shop valued. The original plan was to sell the business premises, but the evaluation was so pathetically low – the bloke didn't know what he was doing – that I had a rethink. I have now come up with the idea of selling the house and keeping the business premises. I am going to lease the building for ten years, until the mortgage is paid. I have advertised on a website called Gumtree. I have told any potential buyers that it will not be available until February, because I have to work until then. I have had some interest already, and this gives me hope. I am going to put the house on the market in October. I live in a popular area and am confident the house will sell quickly.

The next day, I am in work, and it is quiet. I decide to sort out my file cabinet. I keep all important paperwork in here, including keepsakes from the children over the years; the heart Jonah made me and slid under the door is in there. As I sort through the file marked qualifications, I come across Jonah's old school end-of-year book.

There is a personal profile in the front. I read that Jonah has written about his interests and hobbies, as well as his favourite television programmes and films (he lists them with the director's name first). Then I read his comments about his aims, objectives, and goals in life. Jonah has written, "The biggest inspiration in my life is my mother." I am choked. When I visit him the following week, I tell Jonah that I am on a course and need some feedback on what it was like growing with me as his mother. We asks why. I tell him I am writing an essay on working parents for the course. Ten minutes later, he hands me a note and has written this.

Having four children to raise on your own at the age of twenty-four would daunt most people. My mother didn't exactly relish in this scenario, however she ploughed through this task gracefully, making sure we always had food on the table, had the most out of our education, and most of all were happy. She still maintained a drive to make something of herself, and she has achieved ten times more than she could've hoped for.

I look back on my life and realise all the hard work has been worth it.

The results of my IELTS remark have landed on the carpet. It is a week before I leave for my holiday. I open the letter, and the mark remains the same. I am devastated and am exhausted physically and mentally. I decide that when I return from Australia I will rebook the test. I need to forget about it for the moment and rest my brain.

My friends and clients cannot believe that I am travelling alone on my trip. I cannot see what the fuss is about. Secretly, I'm excited at the thought of seeing Drew after nearly two years! It is a week before the holiday, and I have been busy accommodating my regular clients before I leave for my two-week excursion. It has been so busy this week, which has enabled me to pay all the bills and have enough spending money. I have arranged to stay at Jonah and Laura's the night before I leave; they live in the city, and this means that I will not have to worry about catching the train in the morning. I wonder whether Drew will meet me there at the airport, and what it will be like seeing him again.

Departure day has arrived. I have packed well and am organised. I'm wound up and stressed, which I did not expect. Jonah is trying to reassure me that I won't miss the bus, and he has decided to accompany me to the bus station to see me off. We get a taxi, and he waits with me until the bus is due to arrive. He wishes me well and gives me a hug before setting off for work. While I wait for the bus, I text Eligh and Frankie to remind them to look after the house and keep it tidy. I tell them that I love them and will see them when I return. I also text Polly and tell her I will ring her when I arrive.

Polly texts back to tell me she loves me and to take care of myself. She also asks me to take pictures of all the animals I see. I tell her I will.

As I continue to wait for the bus, a man joins the queue, and he starts chatting to me. He tells me he is going to Libya for seven weeks to visit his family, and that he is a Muslim. He comments on all the violence surrounding his faith at the moment and tells me that not all his people are like that. He despises the ones who hide behind his faith to continue murdering innocent people. He asks if I know anything of the Muslim faith, and I tell him I do not because I am a Catholic. I tell him that I sympathise with what he is saying, and I agree with him. He explains that true Muslims believe in the Virgin Mary and Jesus Christ. I admit that I did not know that. He goes on to talk about his faith and tells me

I should read about it and gain more knowledge. I tell him that I will. The bus arrives, and we board, I am thankful and start to relax. I am en route to the airport, and it will take approximately three hours.

We have stopped several times and are told by the driver that this is our last pick-up before heading straight to Heathrow. My adjoining seat is one of few left vacant on the bus. At the last pick-up, a family of four boards and has to seat separately. A man sits next to me, introduces himself as Ken, and he asks where I'm headed. I tell him my destination, and I see by his hat he is travelling to the same place. He has corks all around it and various Australian badges attached. He tells me that they are emigrating today, via the Singapore route. I tell him the reason for my visit is to see where I would like to settle because I have never been to Australia before and have to look at various locations. Ken tells me that his wife and two sons are going to live in a place in called Coffs Harbour. They have friends who live there, and it is a great place to bring up his family.

He gives me good advice on how to exchange large amounts of currency and what companies are safe to do this with. I ask him if he minds that I write the details down, and I get out my notepad and pen. He tells me that he and his wife travelled around the country before they had their children, and they loved the place. I ask him to tell me what it's like there, and he tells me about their culture and way of living. He describes the different areas and how the humidity can be hard to cope with in cities like Adelaide and Perth. I get loads of information from Ken, and I realise that sometimes one meets people for a reason. His stop is before mine because he flies from terminal three. We shake hands and wish each other luck as he and his family exit the bus. I look to say hello to his wife, but she does not look at me. I conclude that she is either a snob or very annoyed at Ken.

My stop is next. I exit the bus and get my bags. I see the Muslim man and ask him which way I need to go. He directs me to the Etihad reception desk and tells me to ask them for directions. I take his advice and thank him before arriving at terminal C, destination Abu Dhabi, where I sit and wait.

Several people arrive and are anxious to be first in line. I sit and read my book. Eventually the security guard removes the entrance bar and tells the queue to check in our luggage. The young couple in front of me looks relieved. I check in my luggage, and I have plenty of time, so I drink a bottle of water and eat a sandwich I prepared at Jonah's before going into the departure lounge. This airport has loads of duty-free shops, but I have been advised not to purchase anything because in Abu Dhabi, I will have it taken off me. I window shop in between reading my book. Finally, it is time to board the plane.

The plane is the biggest I have ever been on. It is ten seats across, and each seat has its own touch screen television, blanket, headrest, and earphones. I settle into my seat and get ready for take-off. This is great! The couple next to me is from Manchester and is going to Sydney to visit their great-granddaughter for the first time, and to also attend a wedding. Their names are Fred and Maureen. Maureen struggles with the touch screen TV, so I offer to help her. I feel like a pro compared to her, and she is very grateful. The hostesses are lovely and feed us throughout the whole flight for free. We are offered drinks, so I ask for wine because I am on holidays!

After fourteen hours, we descend into Abu Dhabi. Fred and Maureen are catching a different flight because they are headed to Sydney, and I'm going to Melbourne. We say goodbye, and I head for my terminal. I have a four-hour wait before boarding for another eight-hour flight. This is stressful but exciting. I board the plane and find my seat. I have concluded that seat number 45C is a window seat and sit down. A moment later, a pair of young backpackers inform me that I am in their seat. I explain that I wasn't sure which was the correct one. The blonde-haired girl informs me that she booked a window seat and knows it is hers. She has attitude! I tell her that's fine; I do not want to argue. I move, and all is well. Blondie's friend introduces herself as Sara and tells me her friend is Jenny. Sara is nice, and she asks me how long am I going to stay in Melbourne. I tell her that I am only going there for a day or so, and I plan to travel around. She tells me they are staying in Melbourne for six months and travelling for six months.

Throughout the flight, Sara and I chat and discuss our reasons for our trip. She tells me she has to get the travel bug out of her system before settling down with her long-term boyfriend and having a family. I wonder how she will cope with Jenny's mood swings; she has abused the staff throughout the whole flight, and I am relieved when she finally falls asleep. Despite my conversations with my fellow passengers, I still manage to watch four films throughout the journey. My favourite one stars Bradley Cooper, mainly because he is in it. As we exit the plane, I say goodbye to Sara and Jenny and wish Sara luck. The pilot has given us advice on various ways to commute into the city. I decide to take the airbus.

I get through departure and pick up my luggage. It is 7.00 a.m. Australian time, and it's cold. I am surprised as I leave the airport. I spot the airbus, quickly purchase a ticket, and jump on. I ring Polly while en route to tell her I have arrived, and she asks if I am OK. I tell her I am, but I'm very tired. She asks if I have seen a kangaroo yet, and I confess that I haven't. I tell her that this place reminds me of Bristol. After saying goodbye to Polly and promising to look after myself, I arrive at the bus station. I enter the city centre and spot a sign telling me I am in Spencer Street. This good news because my hotel is at 300 Spencer Street. Now I need to decide which way to go. I cannot see any numbers on the buildings nearby, so I enter a Subway sandwich bar and ask for directions after purchasing a coffee. The young assistant tells me that my hotel is about a hundred yards up the road. I thank him and head in that direction.

After booking in, I email Drew telling him that I have arrived in Australia. An hour or so later, I get an email back, and Drew asks where I'm staying. I give him my hotel details, and he texts back that he will arrive in five hours;

he's boarding a plane. He asks if I like Chinese food, and I tell him that I do. He says to be ready at 7.00 p.m. because he's taking me out for a meal. I unpack, shower, and get into bed. I set the alarm for 5.00 p.m. This is surreal. I cannot wait to see him, but right now I need my beauty sleep.

I wake up to the alarm, and I am stewed. I have another shower and wash my hair. By 6.30 I am pacing the floor, I decide to act casual and put on the TV. At 7.10 p.m. there is a tap on the door. I open the door, and we both say hello and hug. He asks how I've been, and I tell him I'm OK. We discuss our flights and start talking like old friends. I offer him some wine, and we lie on the bed chatting. After some time, Drew showers, we both change, and he tells me I look beautiful. I reply, "I love it when you say that," and we head out for dinner.

We find a restaurant nearby and order food. We decide to try each other's meals, and if we like it, we will swap dishes halfway through. We do this, but I don't like his dish, so we swap back. After a bottle of red wine, we decide to go to a bar and have a drink. There is a musician singing a song that Drew knows, he starts to sing the lyrics, and we dance to the song. He tells that it is an old Australian song, and the singer is singing it differently, but it is still good. I love dancing with him, but the jetlag is kicking in, making me feel tipsy and tired, so we decide to head back to the hotel. When we get into the room, Drew decides to have another shower. This makes it easier for me to slip under the covers before he enters the room. I have had four children and am conscious of my body. When he comes back, he tells me to move over because he sleeps on the left hand side. I laugh and slide over. Being tipsy makes it less awkward for us both, and it gives me confidence. We spend all night getting to know each other again.

I wake in the morning snuggled up in his arms.

I'm awake first and head to the bathroom. I discover a huge love bite on my neck. I stroke it and remember his touch before washing my hands and snuggling back into bed, pushing into his toned body. I toss and turn because I am awake and want some attention. I wriggle against him until he rouses, and we start all over again. Drew tells me that morning sex is good, and he wasn't expecting it. I get up and make us some coffee before getting back into bed. He spots the love bite and apologises, but I tell him it's OK. We chat about life and work before getting up. We are going to explore the city, and I need to buy a scarf!

We get some breakfast, and the food here is unusual. I ask him why he would have avocado on toast. He tells me it's nice, but I decide on the poached eggs and bacon on soda bread. He has the same, and we admire the view of the city from the second-floor cafe before leaving and jumping on a tram.

We head for Kilma Beach. I am disappointed because it isn't that nice and is very small, plus I cannot see any sharks! Drew laughs at me as I try to look into the water from the pier. There are parrots in the trees, and I take out my camera and take some photos, as I promised Polly.

Melbourne has a mixture of old and new buildings. There are old-fashioned houses with metal balconies amongst skyscrapers. The city centre is very busy, and there is a lot of art and culture here. Drew tells me that if I want to visit the art galleries, I can do that alone because he isn't into that sort of thing; he thinks that people and life *are* art! After travelling the length and breadth of the city via the tram, we decide to get some lunch.

Before we leave the restaurant, Drew gets a call from work. There is a problem, and he has to head back to sort it out. We get back to the hotel, and he books a flight. He tells me to make sure that I do not emigrate for him, but to do it for myself. He also tells me that it's a long time since he has felt like this about anyone, but he cannot commit to me. He asks me to promise him that I will not come here for the wrong reasons. I promise him that I am not, and I mean it. I am doing it for myself and my children.

Drew gives me advice on where to travel next while I'm here, to get the best ideas on where to settle. I thank him, and we hug before he leaves for his flight. I am alone in my room. I email him, tell him to have a safe journey, and thank him coming to see me. I ask him if it's OK if we can still be friends. He emails back, "We will always be friends, but I cannot promise more than that." I thank him for being honest and tell him I'm OK with that. What else can I say? I understand his reasons why and know they are selfless. Sometimes I think I am not meant to be happy and content – I am destined to spend my life alone.

After exploring my hand-written map from Drew and drinking several cups of tea, coffee, and wine, I decide I am leaving Melbourne in the morning and flying to Brisbane. I am going to stay in hostels and have the adventure of a lifetime. I get up to shower and wash and dry my hair. I add the scarf to my outfit to hide the evidence of seeing Drew, and I head to the airport via the airbus. I purchase my ticket to Brisbane, and it is leaving in three hours. It costs two hundred dollars. I arrive in Brisbane after a two-and-a-half-hour flight. It is 7.00 p.m. and is a lot warmer here.

After exiting the airport, I ask a passerby how I get into the city. I am advised to use the train and commute into the city centre. I pay for a ticket and am told the name of the stop to get off. I ask the attendant to write it on the ticket. Then I book my hostel online while en route; it is called X Base. I write down the address on my notepad and ask for advice when I arrive at my stop.

After walking for five minutes, I look up and am relieved to discover my destination. I think, *Well, here goes!* I check in and am given bedding for my two-night stay. After getting out of the lift, I hear a Scottish girl talking outside my room. I use my key card to enter, and there is only a top bunk bed left. I wonder what the hell I am doing and hope that it does not topple over when I climb up the ladder. Luckily it does not, so I make up my bed, sit on it, and open up my bag of supplies. I open a bottle of water and a sandwich and then pull out my book to read.

Five minutes later, the Scottish girl enters the room, she's named Debbie and introduces the rest of the room's occupants. We say hello. Jess is Canadian, and there are two girls from London who are travelling to Fiji in the morning. There's also a Brazilian girl who doesn't speak much English; Debbie tells me that she is teaching her. Debbie and Jess both send me a friend request on Facebook, and I accept. This might not be so bad after all!

Debbie tells me that she has been living in the hostel while she works here. She adds that her friend is arriving tomorrow, and she is going to stay in a hotel and travel around the country with her, showing her the sights. Morning arrives, and Debbie is packing up. She has loads of stuff, so I offer to give her a hand to carry it, and she accepts. We get to her new residence, and she is thrilled with it. I tell her I have to leave, and she offers to show me around Brisbane. I thank her and accept. We walk over the bridge to the south side of the riverbank. I see skyscrapers and office buildings. Farther up the bank, we come across a festival with stalls and a fairground. Debbie tells me that it is Father's Day here, and that is why it is so busy. Children are playing in a pool, and families are having picnics on the riverbank. We sit and have lunch, and Debbie tells me that she is planning on taking her friend to Sydney first to see the Oprah House. Then they're going to Frazer Island and Queensland. Although she is good company and I am grateful for all the advice she has given me. I am eager to explore the city on my own. We make our excuses and say goodbye.

I take the riverboat across after walking along the south side. I discover the shopping malls, lots of market stalls, and a backpackers' bag sale. It is equivalent to car boot sale back home. There are clothes and umbrellas laid neatly in piles along the floor. The area is buzzing with people shopping for something new.

After looking around for a few hours, I decide to head to the supermarket to restock on supplies. I buy a piece of cooked chicken and some pasta, tomatoes, apples, and yogurts. This should last me for a few days. Life is good, and I like it here but would not want to live in the city. I spend another day exploring Brisbane before setting off for my next destination the Gold Coast. Surfers Paradise Hostel, here I come!

I catch a train to the Gold Coast, and it costs eighteen dollars, or about nine pounds. I am told I will be able to get on the free bus into Surfers Paradise at the train station. I board the bus and take photos for Polly. I haven't seen any kangaroos or koalas yet, but I have taken some scenic shots. There are houses here along the river with boats outside. I bet it would cost a fortune to live here. The weather is around twenty-five degrees, and I am wearing shorts; it is much warmer than Melbourne. It takes me a while to find the hostel, and I have to ask for lots of directions to get there. The people are very friendly and helpful here.

Eventually I book into my room. They have a pool here, and I am impressed. I chat to the young boy who works here. He is from Manchester and has been working here for twelve months. I tell him why I am travelling here, and he advises me to speak to Heidi and her husband. They own the hostel, and she moved here about ten years ago. Heidi is really nice and tells me a little about a place called Robina. She tells me she lives there, and it is a lovely rural area not far from the coast. She says that it is hot all year round here, and at Christmastime it is too warm to go to the beach; the locals don't entertain going at that time of year. She also tells me that there is a lot of work here, and my profession will do well here.

I thank her for the advice and go to my room to shower and change before heading to the beach. The beach has white sand as far as the eye can see. It is beautiful here. I walk along the water but do not swim; the red flags are out, and there are guards along the shoreline. I pull out my book and my wine, and after pouring myself a glass in my portable plastic cup I settle down to read.

I stay for two days at Surfers Paradise. On the second evening, I am asked to join in the evening's quiz night. I team up with my roommate and two young men; one is Canadian, and the other is British. I tell them that I am not very good at quizzes, and they tell me not to worry because it's all in good fun. It's a good night, and when it's over, I thank Rachel, my roommate, for asking me.

The next day, I explore the area and go to the beach for the rest of the day. Whilst in town, I book the rest of my travel arrangements. I am heading for Coffs Harbour tomorrow for two days and one night. Then I am going to travel overnight to Sydney for a day and night. I am booked for

Canberra the Capital for two nights before heading back to Melbourne to fly home.

I get up early because my bus is booked for 9.00 a.m. for Coffs Harbour. It takes seven hours to arrive there. I book my hostel en route. I am dropped off at the bus stop, and there are two hostel transport minibuses waiting. I give my name and am told to get into the bus on the left. The driver, a young lad from Chepstow, gives us a tour on the way. He stops on the top of the mountain and asks us to get out and admire the shoreline. The view is spectacular, and he says that one can go whale spotting here, although it is out of season at the moment.

After booking in, I arrive at my room. There is no one there, but I clearly have roommates; the room is a tip. I make up my bed and secure my belongings in my locker before leaving to look around. I cannot sit in this pigsty for another minute. I head along the coast to admire the beach. It is not dark yet, but it is dusk, and I am aware of the light fading. I do not wander too far away.

I walk along the harbour. The boats are very pretty, and I see fish swimming below. I snap them with my camera for Polly, and I also take photos of the harbour and the bay. I look around and am suddenly overwhelmed by loneliness. If there were no people here, I would break down and cry out my heart. As I look out to sea, I feel more alone than I have ever felt in my whole life. I push back my tears and compose myself. I tell myself to man up and grow a pair of fucking balls. I have to make the best of it. I miss Polly and the boys. Drew has not contacted me. I have no one here.

I go back to the hostel and make myself a cup of coffee out of my supplies. I decide to get an early night. My two roommates arrive in the room in the middle of the night; they are American, loud, and brash.

I wake up in the morning and head into town. I have all day here until I get on the bus headed to Sydney at midnight. I book a taxi with the receptionist before leaving to explore. I ask the receptionist whether there is much work in the area, explaining that I will be moving over here with two sons who will need work. She tells me that there is not much work around here, and if there is, it is seasonal. It's a long walk into town, but the scenery is lovely, and I get to walk through the local village on the way and note what facilities are available here. I pass churches, bowling greens, and a skating park for the youngsters. The local town is very pretty, and the roundabouts are decorated with plants and flowers in bloom.

After walking for an hour or so, I get to the town centre and visit the local shopping mall. There is also a local outdoor organic food market. The weather is warm, but I still have to wear my scarf; although the mark is faded, it is not gone altogether. Every time I look at it in the mirror, I think of Drew. I get some supplies of wine and chocolate and some healthy options (apples and nuts), and then I take my book to the beach. It is lovely here, and I am content again. I have grown my pair of balls! I decide to take some selfies. Jonah gave me Laura's selfie stick before I left, and I want to take some pictures of me on the beach.

I settle back down and observe people walking their dogs and admiring the view of the coastline. I see a man walking towards me; he looks like a local because he is wearing a coat. As he passes me, he says hello, and I reply. He tells me his name is George and asks where I am from. He sits down to chat and he tells me that he is a horse dentist. I tell him a little bit about myself as we watch the ocean. Suddenly he tells me he can see dolphins. I ask him where, and he points to the left of the ocean, near the beach. I see them, and they are ducking in and out of the waves. It is a fantastic sight, and we watch them travel up the coast until they disappear around the bay.

George spots a young girl approaching the beach and asks her where she is from. Her name is Helena, and she is from Perth. She sits, and we start chatting. After an hour or so, I decide to leave and head back to the hostel. As I make my excuses and pack up my belongings, the young girl does the same. We part our separate ways. I go back to my room to have a nap. The two American girls are there, and I can overhear them telling a new arrival how they always get discounts on everything, and how jealous their friends are back home because they are here. If I were their friend, I'd be glad to see the backs of them. They add no one likes sharing a room with them because they are both slobs. That is the only believable comment I have heard.

I soon drift off to sleep and I awake around seven thirty. I take a shower, dry my hair, and dress, ready to depart. I go to the kitchen and prepare some pasta, tuna, and tomatoes before sitting in the recreation room for my taxi. I leave for Sydney in one hour.

I say goodbye to the receptionist, who has been helpful, and then head for the bus stop. When I arrive, there is an Australian couple waiting for the same bus. I am glad of this because the bus ends up being over an hour late. There is also a tramp in the corner, sleeping. The couple asks where I am from, and they decide to have a snack and offer me a biscuit. I decline and look at the tramp. I bet he would love a biscuit, but they do not offer him one. Luckily, I think he is asleep. The bus eventually arrives, and I put my luggage on board. Before boarding, I walk over and place a cereal bar on the bench for the tramp. The couple look at me as if I am mad. It is all the food I have on me, and I want him to have it. I travel on the bus overnight and arrive in Sydney at 9.25 a.m.

I have booked a hostel called the Jolly Jester. I have to catch a train from the bus station to arrive in Sydney's city centre. I arrive at King's Cross Station at 10.30 a.m. and find my way to the hostel. I have a small map of the area and find it within an hour. I book in, shower, and dress. I only have one whole day here, so I decide to explore. The hostel manager gives me directions and a map. I thank him and head off to find the Royal Opera House and the botanical gardens, but first I must find the harbour.

I find the harbour, and it is huge. The boats must cost millions. There is a naval base here, and the navy ships are also docked. I take some pictures. I keep walking and find the botanical gardens. There are wild birds, and they are beautiful. I snap some photos and selfies. I turn the corner and see the opera house and the bridge, and I take more selfies. I walk up to the city centre's main shopping mall and wander through the shops before finding a small cafe at which to have some lunch. I message Polly and the boys to update them and reassure them that I'm all right before heading back to the hostel.

I get a little lost, but while en route I spot a cathedral named St Paul's. It is huge and very pretty. I go inside and light a candle for Mam, Dad, and Dillon. I say a prayer and tell them I am thinking of them. As I leave, I look down and see a solitary white feather at my feet.

I keep walking, and it takes me three hours before I find the hostel. My feet are burning. I go to my room and pour a glass of wine. Suddenly I wake up – I must have fallen asleep. It is late, so I undress, get into bed, and check my phone. I have messages from the boys, Polly, Sophie, and Lorna. I reply to them all because it is early evening back home. I tell them that I am OK and am having a good time. Polly asks if I will see Drew before returning home. I tell her probably not. She asks why and says that she thought I wanted to see him. I reply, "Well, you don't always get what you want, do you?" I set my alarm for 7.00 a.m. I have to be at the bus station in the morning because I am heading to Canberra.

I get up early and shower. I do my hair and make-up and dress before packing and heading for the bus station. The bus arrives on time. I arrive early and so have to wait, but I don't mind. While I'm waiting, I notice a lot of tramps here. Young, old, and mentally ill people are wandering the bus station. A tramp with a tattooed face walks up to me and asks me if I am married. I tell him I am. A young lad waiting for the same bus catches the look of relief on my face as the tramp walks away, and we laugh.

The bus trip to Canberra takes eight hours. I have booked my hostel because it has a four-star rating and a pool. The only downside is I could only get a mixed room for the first of my two nights. I am not happy. I arrive at the hostel and ask if there have been any cancellations for a women-only room. They tell me there hasn't been, but they are trying to not book anyone into my room. I thank them, pay, and collect my sheets before heading to my room to shower and change. I enter the room, it is spotless. I am relieved to be the only one here. I come back after a relaxing shower and decide to head to the spa and pool. I take my book, go down, and have a read; it is quiet and no one is in the room. After an hour, I go back to my room. It is still empty, and I am pleased. I change and settle into bed with a much-deserved glass of wine. I eat a yogurt and an apple and read my book.

I am just nodding off to sleep when I hear a key card in the lock of the door. As I compose myself, three young Australian lads enter the room. They look at me and apologise. I reply it's OK because it's a mixed room. We introduce ourselves, and they ask where I'm from. I tell them, and they ask if it's OK if they have a shower. It's Saturday night, and they have come from Wooga Wooga to go out in the city. It has taken them two and a half hours to get here! Within an hour, they have asked permission to put on their music, and they are chatting away and drinking vodka. I have given them fashion advice, and they have told me about where they live. It has seventy thousand occupants and is a farming town. They tell me I should move there. They leave at midnight and return about 5.30 a.m. I hear them enter the room, and they are trying to whisper so as not to wake me. So far these have been my favourite roommates; they are really nice lads.

The next morning, the receptionist explains that the lads are leaving today, and I could be the only one in the room. I decide not to risk it. I move to a women-only room before going out to explore Canberra. I walk towards the lake and see signs for a Floriade Spring Festival. I enter and look around. They have a teenage dance competition, so I sit and watch for a while before going to explore. The smell of the flowers is lovely as I walk through the park. I see a big wheel and stalls, and then I walk around and browse at the stalls. After an hour, I decide to go to the refreshment stall, get a glass of wine, and read my book.

Later, I decide to walk around the lake. It is huge and too far to walk. I walk as far as I can, because the path is blocked; there is no access due to building work. I walk around some condos on the lake and discover a sign advertising an indoor market and a glass factory. I go to have a look. The market sells all types of food, and it smells delicious, so I wander inside and buy a jacket potato and some water. I am not daring enough to try the Chinese dishes. The marketplace is busy with people wandering around. If I lived here, I would buy paintings and vases for my home. They are handcrafted, and there are also beautiful oil paintings for sale.

After the market, I decide to look at the Parliament Building. It takes me around two hours to reach the entrance, and I discover that I can go inside. I look around and take some selfies. I am tired and so head to the cafe inside to order a coffee. It is too strong and bitter, and I struggle to drink it. I leave the building an hour later. I still haven't seen a kangaroo for Polly, and there is no sign of one here. I wonder whether I will spot one on the way back to the hostel. I get a little lost on the way back and end up near a nature reserve and housing estate. After asking several local people, I find my way back to the city centre. I stop at a cafe and order a cake and a cup of tea – I have earned it after all that walking. I spend the evening soaking my poor feet in the pool; they are blistered and sore after getting lost, because it took me over seven hours to get back. After settling back into my room, I go down to the kitchen and prepare my dinner before having an early night.

I spend the next day looking at the shopping mall. My feet are still sore from yesterday, so I do not want to wander too far. I am heading back to Melbourne tomorrow and have decided to stay at the hotel on Spencer Street because it is near the station, and I deserve a treat. I have saved a lot of money by staying in hostels, enjoyed the experience, and met some nice people.

I wake early and head to the bus station. The wheel on my case is breaking, so I get a taxi. I arrive in Melbourne eight hours later. My hotel is like heaven, I have my own shower and toilet, and it is immaculate. I sit and watch television; there is only one English channel, and *Doc Martin* is on. I pour a glass of wine and eat my supper in bed. Tomorrow I will be heading home.

I get up in the morning, enjoy a nice shower, wash and dry my hair, and pack. I leave the room and go for breakfast. I head to the same place at which Drew and I ate. They make the best poached eggs here, and I enjoy every mouthful. Finally I get on the airbus and head for the airport. It is time to head home. In two days, I will be back in work.

I gain about twelve hours on the flight home and arrive at Heathrow at 7.30 a.m. My cases take around an hour to come through the conveyor, and eventually I leave the airport after purchasing a decent cup of tea to wait for my bus home. The Jamaican lady I met on the flight comes over to sit with me while we wait. Within thirty minutes, her son arrives to pick her up. We say goodbye, and she leaves. Ten minutes later, the bus arrives. The driver is miserable, unlike the Australian ones I dealt with over the last two weeks. I load my cases onto the bus and take my seat. I arrive home around 1.30 p.m. after catching a train for the last part of the journey.

Frankie and Eligh have kept the house as clean as two young men can. The dishes are done, so I am happy with that. They are glad to see me, especially because the food supplies are running low. I clean the bathroom, empty my case, and start washing my laundry. I ring my staff, who have covered me while I have been away, to tell them I will be in tomorrow. They tell me there have been no problems while I was away, and this is a relief. Work the next day is a struggle because I am really tired, but I manage to work through the jetlag.

A week after my return, I get an email from Drew. He asks if I had a safe journey home and apologises for not being able to met me a second time. I know he's being polite, and I wonder whether he was scared that he may start to have feelings for me if we met again. Or maybe he simply didn't want to. I text back that it is OK, and that I got home all right. I ask him how work is going and keep the conversation light and casual.

I have learnt over the years that I cannot make someone want me, and I understand why we can never be together. His life is complicated, and I am determined not to spoil the friendship we have. He is my confidant, the only person whom I can really talk to. He gives me good advice, and I trust his judgement. His actions towards me are selfless – one of the reasons why I care for him.

I think about my future. I am going to have to start a new life on my own. When I emigrate, I will be free. I am sure there will be someone out there who will be interested in being with me and will have no emotional ties to anyone else.

It is two weeks since I came home from Australia. I have reapplied to do my IELTS test. I have three weeks to prepare for it, and I am determined to pass with the appropriate grades. I revise every night after work, until my exam day arrives. I am mentally drained and exhausted, and I have had trouble eating and sleeping. Eventually, the day of the exam arrives. I need this test because it is the only thing standing in my way. Three hours later, it is all over. As I leave the building, I am close to tears. I hope I have passed it. I rush back to work; it is a Saturday, and I have booked clients. I finish work at 6.30 p.m. and then head to the shop and buy a bottle of red wine.

The following two weeks are spent filling my time by decorating the house. If I could take a week off work, it would be OK, but I cannot afford to do so. After work each night, I paint. I start with my bedroom and then complete the landing and stairs, the living room, the dining room, and finally the kitchen and the bathroom ceiling. I paint every door throughout the whole house and complete all the glossing.

It is the day that my IELT results are due. I decide to ring the office. A member of staff informs me that the results will be online at one minute before midnight tonight. I keep working until 11.55 p.m., and then I reluctantly set up my laptop to view my results. I am so nervous that I open a bottle of wine and pour myself a glass before pressing the button to reveal my results. I am afraid to look but do it anyway. I passed! I am so pleased to receive a 9.0 speaking, 8.5 writing, 7.5 reading, and 8.0 listening, for a total score of C2. I am so chuffed that I email Drew to tell him, as well as Sophie, Polly, and Jonah. They text back well done, and they knew I could do it. Yes!

I email my results to the emigration service, and the next day I get a reply of, "Well done!" The following weekend, I order gravel for the garden – five tonnes of it! My next job is to weed, line, and cover the garden with gravel. The house is booked to go up for sale in five days. It is back-breaking work, but I am determined to complete it. I continue even when my back is in half and screaming at me to stop. I have taken all the garden rubbish to the skip, and the garden is finished. Exhausted is not even close to how tired I feel, but I am proud of myself. I have also had carpets fitted in the living room and my bedroom to finish the inside of the house.

The estate agent arrives the next day. I have spent the morning planting all my pots in order to finish the desired look of the garden. He values the house at £140,000. If it sells at that price, I will have made £40,000 on the property. This will be enough to settle all my bills and pay off both mortgages on the house and the shop. This means I can use the rental income from the shop to cover my rental expenses in Australia.

It is a month before Christmas, and the shop is already booking up. I am aware that this is going to be my last one in the shop, and I am feeling nostalgic. I am also aware that I have to make as much money as possible before I hand over the business to the new business owner, to ensure that I can afford the flights and visas.

The month of December goes quickly. I have decided to make the most of the house now that it is finished, and I am enjoying living there for as long as I can before it sells. I love the completed living room; it is warm, cosy, and everything I wanted to achieve. I put up the tree, and it finishes the look of the room. I have given my tenant two months' notice on the flat. I need the property to store my belongings, and for me and the boys to live in just in case the house sells quickly. Most of my income for the shop is spent on bills and Christmas presents for the children. Lorna and her husband are coming for Christmas lunch, as well as Jonah, Eligh, Frankie, Polly, and Eric. I am happy that they are all coming for our last Christmas in this house. I have planned to tell Lorna and Andy after Christmas day is over with; I do not want to upset them before it.

Work has been extremely busy. This is good, although I am shattered. I have also managed to achieve my ILM degree in business leadership and management level five, on my target date. Although I am pleased because everything is going to plan, I am also exhausted and feel burnt out. However, me being me, I have still managed to book a few nights out with friends and family. I have arranged a night out with Lorna and Sophie and two friends.

It is a week before Christmas. I pick up Lorna as planned, and we meet Sophie and the girls in the local pub. On the way, Lorna tells me that she had a weird conversation with the shop owner next to mine. She tells me that she asked her if Polly and Eric were coming home, because the lady who rents the flat told her she had been given notice for personal reasons. I am furious that she is a nosy old bat! I am not ready to tell Lorna yet, but have promised myself that I will not lie to her.

I tell her that of course they aren't moving home. This is true. She asks if I have told the tenant to leave. I change the subject and rant on about the nosy old bat and how I wish she would mind our own business. We arrive at the pub, I park the car, and we go to meet the others.

A few hours later Lorna asks me if I have given the tenant notice again. She won't leave the subject go! I tell her "yes I have, I say that it's because I am struggling to pay two mortgages and I am thinking of selling the house and moving into the flat".

Lorna replies, "I was thinking that now that you have achieved your degree, why don't you teach full-time? This will mean that you can get proper holidays." I decide now is the time, so I take a deep breath and tell her. I remind her that I have brought up four kids on my own, and I want to do something for myself and the two boys who are living at home. I have decided to go to Australia for a year to give them a good start in life and a better chance of career prospects. She looks at me and tells me she doesn't want me to go. She is not happy about it.

We have both had a few drinks now and are feeling tipsy. I reply I am doing something for me for a change, and I want her to understand and be happy for me. Before we can say anything else, the girls and Sophie arrive back from the bar. I am secretly relieved, but I hope that it won't ruin Christmas lunch, and that she and Derick don't question the children too much.

It has been nearly a week since I told Lorna. She has pretended I haven't said anything, and it is weird. It is Christmas Eve, the best day of the year for me. After work, I head home. Jonah has arrived and is drinking a can of lager already. Laura has gone to stay with her mother so that she is not alone for Christmas Day. I prepare the vegetables and cook the meat for the next day. Later on, Polly and Eric arrive. They have decided to stay at Eric's parents' for tonight, which means that Jonah can sleep in the spare room. It is great to have everyone home, and we have a nice evening watching films, eating, and drinking. The house is busting at the seams, and I love it!

Christmas Day is here! I wake Jonah and Frankie. Eligh is in the attic bedroom, so Jonah pops his head up to wake him. We exchange presents before visiting Sophie and her brood. I then visit Andy and his family before heading back to the house to prepare a feast. Polly and Eric, along with Lorna and Derick (my brother-in-law), arrive at 1.30 as planned. Jonah acts as barman and offers refreshments whilst I see to the dinner and lay the table.

Lorna goes into the living room to talk to the boys. I can hear her laughing at a tale Jonah is telling her. Lorna's husband, Derick, comes into the kitchen and asks me if it's true that I am going away. I tell him what I told Lorna. He replies, "Oh, well, don't talk about it today, then. Lorna is very upset." I tell him that I won't. Three hours later, dinner is done and consumed, and all the crackers have been pulled before Sophie and her brood arrive. I serve desserts to everyone, and the drink is flowing. We all have a good laugh as one big, happy family. I make plans to go out with Sophie and Lorna on Boxing Day before they leave for home. We are going to our local and meeting there at 4.00 p.m. The boys and Polly have made their own plans for the day.

We arrive in the pub the next day and get some drinks. The first hour is quiet, but it eventually fills up, and soon we are chatting to loads of old friends. By 7.00 p.m. Sophie has been picked up and gone home. Lorna and I are now on double vodka and Cokes and are drunk. I am introduced to a man called Simon, and he tells me all about himself and says that he has been down lately, so his friends encouraged him to come out for a drink. Within the next hour, he has told all about his life and is flattering my ego. I end up letting him walk me home, and we arrange a date for the following night.

Simon takes me to the pictures, and then we go back to his for a coffee. The coffee turns into a glass of wine, and we chat into the late hours, so I end up staying the night. Simon is a nice bloke, and we get on. I am worried because he tells me he likes me. I do not want to get too attached to anyone. I will be leaving for Australia in a few months, so this is not the time to meet Mr Right.

Within the next week, I have seen Simon five times! This is a record for me. He has already asked me if I plan to remarry, and he has also been talking about when we tell his friends and family about us. He's even calling me his girlfriend! I tell him to slow down because I don't want to end up hurting him. He replies, "How will you do that?" I tell him that I am going away – I am emigrating. He looks hurt but tells me that this has been the best Christmas he has had in years. He has seen how his life could be, and he says that after living through the last year with depression and the stress of selling his house and moving, he is happy to take this for what it is and enjoy what time we have together. He says he enjoys my company and asks if we can continue to date until I leave. I agree as long as it is at my own pace, and he stops rushing me.

Secretly, I am worried and tell Jonah that I have visions of him hanging off my leg as I'm getting on the plane. What should I do? There is a part of me that likes him and the attention I get, but another part of him scares me. Lorna is pleased – I know she thinks if I meet a man, I won't go. She is wrong. Going away is not about meeting a man; it is about changing my way of life. I am going even if I end up falling for Simon.

Drew messages me and wishes me a Merry Christmas and Happy New Year. I wish him the same. I could never give up his friendship. On 4th January I am starting the first week back in work. In five weeks, I will be handing over my business to the new owner. Time is going so fast, and I still need to hear about my visa before I can book flights and start to arrange the trip. I also have to get the house sold and move into the flat. It is going to be a hard four months!

I am seeing Simon tomorrow and will get my accounts up to date on Wednesday. The accounts take a week to complete, and I am tired and cannot face paperwork. This is a job I will not miss!

Every day counts now, and I cannot waste time dating, but the need to confide in someone and feel loved is making me stick with Simon. Polly's advice is to give him a chance; she has told me that he probably just likes me. Jonah and Laura have told me to be on my guard because Simon's coming on a bit heavy. They all have my best interests at heart. I am confused and so have decided to keep the dates to two a week.

Luckily, work has been busy, and this means I can save and pay the monthly bills. I have been dating Simon for two weeks now. This is a record for me. He has taken my advice and cooled off, making him more attractive to me. Simon is everything I would have wanted in a man two years ago. He is kind, caring, and considerate in every way. He compliments me on my figure, although I know it is not perfect, and he tells me how much he fancies me on a daily basis. Although he has said he wants to date me until I leave and live for today, I am worried that I am going to hurt him badly. I have been introduced to his friends and some of his family. They are nice people and do not know I am leaving for a new life. Simon doesn't want them to know this information because he knows the advice they will give him is to leave me before he gets hurt. I worry that I am being selfish.

I text Drew and ask him advice about the move and the cost of the rent over there, to give me a rough idea of how much things will cost. I do not want to tell him about Simon. Drew texts me with this information, and we reminisce about our dates together. He tells me he misses that. I remind him of our date in Australia. He replies that he is going out for dinner. It sounds as if he is going alone, but I don't ask him to confirm it. I wonder where his partner is, and my gut instinct is that things are not working out for him. If they were, why would he be texting me and telling me he misses our times together? I know if I had to choose between Simon or Drew, it would be Drew; that is where my heart is. Several hours later, Drew texts me, telling me that he is home now and going to bed. He texts, "Goodnight, beautiful." It's morning here, but I wish him a goodnight. I have a date with Simon tomorrow and must put Drew out of my head. Simon does not need to know about him. It is not cheating because Drew is my friend, nothing more. I am not going to feel guilty about it. Sometimes what you don't know can't hurt you.

A week later, I hear about my visa application from the lady at the migration company. She has sent it off for the final stage, which will take around twelve weeks. She has told me that every year the migration company lists the eligible locations that I will be allowed to apply for, depending on my occupation. I have the choice of three destinations: Northern Territory, South Australia, or Tasmania. I text Drew for advice and tell him I do not want to live anywhere tropical. He texts back the next day: Northern Territory is out, so I have to choose between SA and TAS.

It takes me two days to decide where I am going to live. I chose Adelade because it is cooler there. Drew tells me that it is a great place to live and has a lot of British people living there. The lady at the migration company is sorting out working visas for the boys and finding me employment so that I do not have to worry about looking for work when I get there. I text Polly and Eric and then Jonah and Laura to tell them the news and get them to book holidays from work, to ensure they will be able to come. I have to keep enough money to pay for flights, visas, and insurances, as well as spending money. My budget is tight, but I think I will be able to manage it. I need the house to sell!

A month later, I get some good news. I get an offer on the house, but it is below the asking price by five thousand pounds. I think about the offer for a few days before deciding to accept it. Now I need the tenant in the flat to pull her finger out and move out. Then I will be able to move in with the boys and sort things out. The salon has been taken over by the new owner, and he has decided to keep me on until I leave. This is good news for me because I still have an income.

I am still dating Simon, and he is smitten. I care for him, but it's not enough to keep me here. I am seeing him three times a week now and enjoy our nights together. We go to the pictures or out for meals, and then we go back to his place and stay up most of the night, talking. He is a nice man, and I will miss him. Simon tells me this is the happiest he has been in a long time, and then he adds that he loves me. I jokingly tell him that I will be dragging him on my leg across the airport runway as I am boarding the plane. He tells me to bugger off and calls me a cheeky cow! Still, we both worry that this is true.

Time flies as I make all the arrangements to go away. Laura cannot get time off work. This means that Jonah will come alone, and they will return in the summer holidays to visit again when she has her annual holidays. I know I am being selfish, but I cannot give up Simon. |Drew texts me, and I reply when I am not with Simon. He is lonely; I can tell by the way he reminds me of our time together. I tell him that I miss him, and I mean it. They are two different men, and I am having completely different relationships with them.

My customers are happy for me but sad to see me go. Most of them have become friends over the years. I will even miss the moany old regulars. I am leaving in three weeks Sophie is happy for me and plans to visit. Some of my friends have already decided they are going to visit me. I have joked that I will have to have a rota. Lorna hasn't spoken about it. I know she is devastated, but I have to do this; for once, it's about me. Andy was surprised but has taken it well. His advice was, "Don't regret the things you do, but the things you don't." He wishes me luck and tells me to go for it. I am pleased that he is happy for us; it is a relief. I know he will miss me because Sophie and Lorna rarely visit him. I hope that my sisters will take the time to see him more often.

The house sells, and I have moved into the flat. This is very handy for work. I have been able to clear the mortgage on the shop with the equity I gained on the sale of the house, leaving me with enough money to comfortably start my new life in Australia. It takes a full twelve weeks for the visas to arrive. Eligh has finally come to terms with the move and is willing to give it a try. I have had farewell nights out with family and friends for over a month. Simon hasn't come because he is finding it hard to cope. He has suggested visiting and keeping our relationship long-distance. I have agreed to this to keep him happy, but I don't think it will work. Secretly, I am relieved that he has children that are tying him to Britain, because I know otherwise he would be packing a bag and coming with me. The boys would not want that, and neither would I. I am doing this for a fresh start, and although I care for Simon, I always knew the relationship was not permanent for me. I feel selfish for thinking this way. Simon has been nothing but kind and caring to me, but he is not Drew.

I have managed to get Lorna to come to terms with the move over the last week. I have included her in visits to see Jonah and Laura. While en route, we have had time to talk about me going away. She cries and confesses that not being able to have children has affected her over the years. If someone asks her if she would like a child now, the answer would be no, but now that she is going through menopause and has been told she can't have them, and it is final, she is devastated. I remind her that when she had the chance to see about fertility treatment years ago, Derick would not consider it.

I tell her that she only has one life and that she chose Derick over having a family. I remind her that she was happy with that decision. She also tells me that with me going away will mean that she will not be able to see my children as well. I remind her that she has never invited any of us to her house, ever. I tell her that we were never welcome because Derick wanted it that way, and I remind her that she always stood by his decision.

What does she expect Polly and Eric or Jonah and Laura to do if they visit her? Stand outside her garden gate for a chat? Her reply to this is that her house is messy. I comment that so is Sophie's, but we have all always been welcome there. We are not snobs and would not comment on the state of her home, and she knows that.

She agrees to my reasons for leaving, but she thinks I will never return. I tell her she is welcome to visit me. She stubbornly refuses, telling me that her dog would pine to death if she left him for that long. I tell her that although I do not wish her dog any harm, if he dies, she then has no excuse. I realise how different we are, and really, it is always going to be all about poor Lorna. She will never understand just how hard my life has been.

Three days later, Lorna and I go to Bingo for a night out. On the way, she tells me if I leave her the flat key, she can look after the place for me, just in case there is a burst pipe or something. I tell her I am leaving keys with Polly and Eric. She adds, "But if I need somewhere to go to have a break from Derick, I can use the flat. Yes, that will be good." Later that night, I tell Polly and Simon. Both are in agreement that I am not doing that. I wonder whether Lorna will miss me or whether she just wants my house and the business premises!

It is the night before I am due to leave and start my new life in Australia. We are all in the flat, and the adventure has nearly begun. Family and friends are meeting us in the local pub in the morning to see us off before the minibus arrives to take us to the bus station. The farewells are painful, and as I turn to get onto the bus, I see Simon. He is crying, so I go over and hug him. I can't stop the tears falling. I kiss him and tell him he will be OK, adding I will contact him when I get there. He whispers that he loves me. I reply, "You too." I cannot say it back because I don't love him. I do care about him and do not like seeing him hurt. I get on the bus, and we head to the airport. I wonder if I have lost the only chance I will ever have to be loved. I am leaving behind family and great friends, but I will come back and visit. Simon will meet someone new and be happy.

The adventure has begun. My new life is a day away. The flights are long, and everyone is moaning. I am excited and want to show Eligh and Frankie a new way of life. This is going to be the best adventure of our lives. In the airport, I get an email from Drew asking me when I will be arriving. I tell him I am fourteen hours away. I get messages from Simon asking how the flight is going and telling me he misses me already. Family and friends are wishing us well on Facebook.

Fifteen hours later we land at Adelade Airport. Everyone is tired, but we are excited to have arrived. It takes too long to get our luggage. As we leave the airport, I notice someone holding a card with my name on it. It says, "Lauren Francis: Good Day and Welcome to Australia!" It's Drew! Maybe there is a chance for us after all.

New Beginnings

Lauren embraces her new life, and her adventure begins. Along with hard work and determination, she finds the hope she needs to succeed and achieve her dreams. Throughout her journey, she experiences love, heartache, friendships, and a lot of laughs along the way. She finally realises she is the only person who can turn around her life.

Lightning Source UK Ltd.
Milton Keynes UK
UKOW03f0256280117
293085UK00001B/4/P